W9-CCP-760

By Martha Grimes

～◦～

The Man with a Load of Mischief
The Old Fox Deceiv'd
The Anodyne Necklace
The Dirty Duck
Jerusalem Inn
Help the Poor Struggler

Help the Poor Struggler

MARTHA GRIMES

A DELL BOOK

Published by
Dell Publishing Co., Inc.
1 Dag Hammarskjold Plaza
New York, New York 10017

To Leon Duke,
who leant a hand

and Mike Mattil,
who helped a poor struggler

Her mind lives tidily, apart
From cold and noise and pain,
And bolts the door against her heart,
Out wailing in the rain.

— Dorothy Parker

O, man, dear, did ya never hear
Of pretty Molly Brannigan?
She's gone away and left me
And I'll never be a man again;
Not a spot on me hide
Will the summer sun e'er tan again,
Now that Molly's gone and left me
Here for to die.

— Irish folk song

CONTENTS

PROLOGUE

THE little girl stood in her flannel nightdress holding the telephone receiver. She carefully dialed the numbers her mother always did when she wanted the operator.

A silky-haired cat at her feet arched its back, yawned, and began washing its paw as the little girl waited through several *brr-brr*'s for the operator to answer. Maybe they didn't wake up until late, the little girl thought. Her mum always said they were lazy. She looked out the leaded glass window almost lost under its thatch collar to see it just pearling over with early-morning light and the moorland beyond floating in morning mist. There was a spiderweb with beads of dew between the thatch and the window. The *brr-brr* went on. She counted ten of them and then hung up and picked up the phone again. The cat leapt to the table to sit and watch the spider painstakingly finish its web.

Bloody operators. That was what her mum always said, sitting here at the table, looking out like the cat, over the blank face of the moor that surrounded their hamlet. The phone kept *brr*-ing. The veil of gray light lifted like a delicate curtain drawn back showing the far horizon where a line of gold spun like the spiderweb.

There was a click, and someone answered. Her voice seemed to come from a great distance, as if she were calling across the moor out there.

The little girl held the black receiver with tight hands and tried to speak very clearly because if they didn't like you they'd just hang up. That's what her mother'd always said. *The cheek of them. Think they're the bloody Queen, some of them.* Her mother spent a lot of time on the telephone and slammed it down a lot.

"My mum's dead," she said.

There was a silence and she was afraid the operator was going to hang up, like the Queen. But she didn't. The operator asked her to repeat what she'd just said.

"My mum's dead," the little girl said patiently, despite her fright. "She never died before."

Now the operator sounded much closer — not way off across the moor — and was asking her questions in a nice tone of voice. What was her name and where did she live?

"My name's Tess. We live in the moor." *This bloody moor,* her mother had always said. She'd hated where they lived. "My mum's in the kitchen. She's dead."

Last name?

"Mulvanney."

The cat's white fur gleamed in the newly risen sun. The spiderweb was spangled with diamond-dew, and as Tess tried to answer the operator's questions the web broke and the spider — it was a tiny brown spider — hung on a silver thread. The cat's tail twitched. The operator was saying they must live in a certain *place* in the moor. A village? And what was their telephone number?

"Clerihew Marsh," said Tess, looking down at the dial. She told the operator the number there. "She's in the kitchen and she won't get up. I thought she was playing. Are you going to call the hospital and will the ambulance come?"

The operator was very nice and said, Yes, of course. She told Tess maybe her mum wasn't dead at all, just sick, and they'd get the doctor. The operator told her very clearly *not* to hang up, that she'd call someone and get back to Tess straightaway.

Silence again. The operator was being very nice, but the operator hadn't been in the kitchen and didn't understand. The cat wore a halo of light, and the spider was repairing its web with infinite patience.

When Tess heard the operator's voice again, she tried to explain: "I thought she was playing with my fingerpaints. We have paints at school. I thought she got the red pot." The operator asked her what she meant. "There's red all over the kitchen. She's cut. It's blood. It's on her dress and in her hair."

Quickly, the operator told her again not to hang up, that she had to call someone else. Soon she was back and talking to Tess in a soothing voice about things like school. Yes, said Tess, she went to school. They called it babies' school, but she wasn't a baby. She was five years old. She told the operator about her teacher, who looked like a toad. They talked a long time and Tess figured out why the operators hardly ever answered. They were talking to people.

The cat yawned and jumped from the table, and Tess knew it wanted its breakfast and would wander into the kitchen. "I've got to hang up. I don't want Sandy — that's our cat — to go into the kitchen." Tess hung up.

Rose Mulvanney lay beneath the kitchen table, her legs jackknifed, her dress blood-besotted. Blood had splattered the kitchen floor, the white daub walls, and even the low, dark beam of the ceiling.

Teresa Mulvanney wondered how it had got up there. She shook and shook her head, forgetting everything as her mind drifted and filmed over. She closed her eyes and scratched her elbows. What must be happening was that she was having one of her "bad" nights; she was dreaming. It must all be paint, after all, or tomato ketchup. Her mother, Rose, had said that in films they used that. Tess, with her eyes still closed, told her mother it was all right and she could get up now. It was a game and it was all a dream anyway. Even the *brr*-ing of the telephone and the far-off double note that made her think of ambulances came as dark figures in fog. She began to hum a song that Rose Mulvanney used to sing when Teresa was a baby.

She forgot to feed the cat.

When Detective Inspector Nicholson and Sergeant Brian Macalvie of the Devon-Cornwall constabulary got to the small cottage in Clerihew Marsh, Teresa Mulvanney was humming and writing her name on the white wall in her mother's blood.

Brian Macalvie had never seen anything like it and he never forgot it. At this time he was twenty-three years old and was generally thought to be the best CID man in the whole Devon-Cornwall constabulary. It was an opinion held by practically everyone, even Macalvie's enemies — also practically everyone. He was not fond of taking orders; he was always talking about his Scots-Irish-American ancestry and dying to get out of England; he was always getting promoted.

He worked on the murder of Rose Mulvanney even after the file had been officially closed. Three months after the Mulvanney murder, they'd arrested (according to Macalvie) the wrong man — a young medical student who lived in Clerihew Marsh and went to Exeter University. He'd been arrested on flimsy, circumstantial evidence — he'd had a heavy crush on Rose Mulvanney, fifteen years older, and, being a medical student, he knew how to use a knife. The motive was unrequited love; the evidence (said Macalvie), Nil.

During the same period, he moved in on six other cases that he felt the department was snailing along on and solved those, so that it was difficult for the divisional commander to tell him to get off the Mulvanney case. Macalvie was his own police force. When he walked into the lab, the pathologists and technicians clung to their microscopes. It was Macalvie's contention their fingerprint expert couldn't find a bootprint on a hospital sheet. If it came down to it, the whole department couldn't find a Rolls-Royce if it was parked in front of the Moorcombe headquarters on Christmas Day.

Thus when the divisional commander told him to get off the Mulvanney case, that the case was closed, Macalvie dropped his ID on the table and said, "Macalvie, six; Devon-Cornwall, Nil." He wasn't halfway across the room before his superior's tone changed. As long as Macalvie didn't let the Mulvanney business interfere with his other duties . . .

"Tell that to Sam Waterhouse," said Macalvie, and walked out.

Sam Waterhouse was the medical student who had been sent to Dartmoor prison. It was a life sentence with the possibility of parole, since there were no prior convictions and the murder of Rose Mulvanney was judged a *crime passionel.*

Macalvie had not hesitated to let the Devon-Cornwall constabulary feel the full weight of his personal displeasure. They had ruined the kid's life and, possibly, a brilliant career.

And if there was one person who knew about brilliant careers, it was Brian Macalvie.

The tiny hamlet of Clerihew Marsh was nothing more than a few fat cottages huddled on either side of a curving road, giving the distorted image of dwellings reflected in a pier glass or a fun-house mirror. After the first clump of houses, so stuck together they looked as if they shared the same thatched roof, the cottages straggled a little, like a sleeve unraveling. The Mulvanney cottage was the last in the fringe. It sat by itself, windows on every side, quite visible to anyone passing.

But apparently no one had been when Rose Mulvanney was being cut with a knife. No one had seen anyone go in or out. No one had seen any strangers about. No one had heard anything. No one who knew him believed Sam Waterhouse could do such a thing.

Macalvie followed every conceivable lead — there were few enough — down to the milk-float man, and had the little wren of a woman who ran the sub-post office chirping nearly daily about the way Rose bought her food. Macalvie had browbeaten the teacher of the Infant's School into delivering up her small quota of information about Teresa Mulvanney. Nor was he beyond using the same tactics with the odd school chum if he could collar one. The headmistress finally complained to the Devon-Cornwall police.

One of the most important persons in the case, one he had not questioned initially, was Rose's older daughter. She'd been away on a school trip when the little sister had made the awful discovery.

She'd come bursting into Macalvie's office, a lanky kid of fifteen with toothpick arms and no breasts and long hair. She'd stood there with fire in her eyes and yelling at him, spattering obscenities like blood on his office walls. Her baby sister, Teresa, had been taken to hospital. Teresa was catatonic. All she did was lie on her cot, curled up like a baby, sucking her thumb.

It was as though Macalvie had been sitting in a warm bath of his own infallibility (it never occurred to him he wouldn't come up with the answers), and this kid had come along and pulled the plug. She got so hysterical she slammed her arm across the stuff on his desk, sending papers, pens, and sour coffee cups all over the floor.

He never solved the case; he never forgave himself; he never saw the kid again.

Her name was Mary Mulvanney.

Twenty Years Later . . .

෴

I

The Alley by the Five Alls

ONE

SIMON Riley never knew what hit him.

That was, at least, the opinion of the medical examiner called to the scene by the Dorset police. The wound in the boy's back had been administered very quickly and very efficiently by a knife honed to razor sharpness. The pathologist agreed and added that, given the angle of the downward thrust, the knife had been wielded by someone considerably taller than Simon. That didn't help the Dorset police greatly, since Simon had been a twelve-year-old schoolboy and was wearing, at the time of his death, the black jacket and tie which constituted the school uniform. That the killer was at least a foot taller would not be particularly helpful in establishing identity.

The boy lay face downward in the alley by the Five Alls pub, crumpled in fetal position against the blind wall which was the pub's side facing the alley. Scattered around the body were a ten-packet of John Players Specials and a copy of *Playboy*. Simon had been indulging in every schoolboy's twin sins — smoking fags and looking at naked women — when the killer had come up behind him. This was the construction of Detective Inspector Neal of the Dorset police, and there was no reason to think it inaccurate.

It was the kitchen girl at the pub, opening the side door of the Five Alls to toss a bag in the dustbin, who had been unlucky enough to find him on that awful evening of February tenth. She had come in for some stiff questioning and had had to be sedated.

The Five Alls was a tucked-away place on a Dorchester side street. The squinty little alley where the boy had been found dead-ended on a blank wall. For Simon Riley's secretive pastimes, it was well located. Unfortunately for Simon, it was just as well located for murder.

TWO

RILEY's. Fine Meat and Game. Superintendent Richard Jury and Detective Sergeant Alfred Wiggins looked through the shop window at their own reflections superimposed over the hanging pheasants. The shop was (a sign announced) licensed to sell game. A young man and an older one were serving a queue of women who were armed with wicker baskets and string bags. From the description given Jury, he took the older man to be Albert Riley himself, the boy's father. It was two days after Simon's body had been found and one day before his funeral. Jury was a little surprised to see the boy's father working.

Apparently, best British beef was in strong demand and short supply, given the way the drill-sergeant eyes of the line of women followed Jury's and Wiggins's progress to the front of the queue. There were mutterings and one or two astringent voices telling these two interlopers where the end of the line was just in case they were blind.

When Jury produced his identification, the young man's face went as white as that part of his apron which was still unblotched. Then he turned to the master-butcher, who was defatting some pork chops with swift and measured strokes. It was an unpleasant reminder of the autopsy performed on his son. Riley's knife stopped in midair when his underling turned him toward the Scotland Yard policemen.

Riley handed over the pork chops to the youth as the women behind Jury and Wiggins passed the information along like buckets of water in a fire brigade. Scotland Yard. Jury realized that Riley's fine meat and game might be even more popular today; murder usually had that effect.

Simon's father wiped his hands on a cloth and removed his apron. His thick spectacles magnified his small eyes and made his round face rounder. He was soft-spoken and apologetic, clearly embarrassed at being caught working in such dreadful circumstances. The authority with which he'd used the knife was completely lost when he put it down.

"Shop was closed yesterday," he said. "But I thought I'd go mad, what with pacing up and down and the wife — that's Simon's stepmother — yelling her head off." While saying this, he was leading them to a door at the rear of the shop. "Suppose you think it's cold-blooded, me working —"

Wiggins, seldom given to irony, said, "Not our business to wonder whether it's hot or cold, sir. Just that it's blood."

Riley winced as he led them up a twisting staircase. "Scotland Yard. I told the wife to leave off with that Queen's Counsel person of hers. Told her Dorset police could handle —" Then, seeming to feel he'd made a blunder, he quickly added, "Expect they need all the help they can get. We keep this flat over the shop. Have another house, but this is handy. The wife'll make a cuppa. I could do with something stronger myself."

The "something stronger" was Jameson's and the wife was not at all inclined to make a cuppa. Although it was lunchtime, she was more interested in whiskey than in lunch or tea. Her own hand didn't shake as she downed her drop, but her husband's did, as if he had palsy. When Riley took off his glasses to pinch the bridge of his nose, Jury saw the eyes were red-rimmed — from tears, probably. Mrs. Riley's were red, too, but Jury supposed that was owing more to the bottle than to bereavement. Since she was not the natural mother, she might have thought that released her from weepy demonstrations.

Beth Riley was a big, brassy woman; her face would have done better with a simple hairstyle than with the florid waves, red-rinsed, that framed the head. She was better-spoken than her husband, even given her lubricated voice. The Jameson's had already got a workout.

"Beth insisted on getting that Q.C. in London to call you people —"

"It's just as well *one* of us knows someone in high places." She turned to Jury. "Leonard Matching, Q.C. He's to stand for Parliament in Brixton." From the vague reports Jury had got of mealymouthed Matching, he doubted very much if Brixton would stand for him. The only reason Jury and Wiggins were here was that an assistant commissioner was a personal friend and had handed the request down the line to Chief Superintendent Racer, who had wasted no time in deploying Jury to the provinces. Too bad (Jury imagined Racer thinking) it was only a hundred and sixty-odd miles from London and the old market town of Dorchester rather than Belfast. Jury could just guess how much Inspector Neal enjoyed having his authority presumed upon, but Neal was too much of a gentleman to make Jury's life hell. Many would have.

". . . and not two decent relations to rub together," Beth Riley was saying in a shocking display of acrimony. The child was dead. What had family connections to do with it?

"All right, all right, pet," said Riley, in some attempt to

shush her. Though why the father should have to minister to the totally unfeeling stepmother, Jury couldn't say. Indeed, he couldn't see the two of them together at all, if it came to that. She lost no chance to remind him of her superior education, and Jury simply let her get it out of her system as his eye traveled the room. Over the fireplace were photographs that might bear out her claim, for all its coldness. There was even one of those mahogany coats-of-arms that tourists seemed forever gathering in the race for their roots; there were also framed documents, one with a seal.

"I'm sorry to intrude upon your grief," said Jury to Mrs. Riley. His tone was icy. "But there are a few questions."

Beth Riley sat back, said nothing, left the question-and-answer period up to her husband. Simon had been (she reminded Jury) *Albert's* son.

"Had you remembered anything at all since you talked to Inspector Neal, Mr. Riley? About your son's friends . . . or enemies?" Predictably, Riley disclaimed any enemies — how could a lad of twelve have enemies? It was true the Dorset police had established to their satisfaction that Simon Riley had neither. He was not popular with his schoolmates, but neither was he hated. Nor did anyone seriously believe a schoolboy would be carrying the sort of knife around Dorchester that had inflicted the wound.

Inspector Neal had looked almost unhappier than the father himself when Neal had said *psychopath.* What else could it be? *You know what that means, Superintendent. Child-killer. In Dorchester?*

I wouldn't like it much in London, either, Jury had thought.

". . . psychopath." Albert Riley echoed the word of Inspector Neal. He was wiping his eyes with a much-used handkerchief. Jury's feeling about Riley had changed when he realized that the man probably did have to work to keep from crumbling. Certainly, he was getting no support from his wife.

But with Neal's and Riley's verdict upon who killed Simon, Jury did not agree. The single wound in the boy's back was clean, neat, quick — not the multiple stab-wounds one might have expected from a person who was out for blood or boys. There had been no molesting of the body. This was all Jury had to go on, but he still thought the murder was probably premeditated and that it was Simon — not just any child — the killer had been tracking. According to Neal's report, Simon's mates — though not close ones — hadn't known he stopped in that alley to smoke fags and look at dirty pictures. Thinking of it that way, the wrong questions were perhaps being asked. Certainly, it was possible the boy had an "enemy." It was also possible that the Rileys themselves had.

He did not pose that question at the moment. All he said to Riley was that he wasn't convinced the boy's death was the work of a deranged mind.

Riley looked utterly astonished. "What other reason could there be? You sound like you think someone wanted to — murder *Simon*."

"I could think of half a dozen, Mr. Riley. They could all be wrong, of course." Jury allowed Mrs. Riley to give him another shot of Jameson's, more to keep her in a comradely mood than because he wanted a drink. Beth seemed actually curious about other reasons. She perked up a bit. Jury found her curiosity and perkiness as depressing as the gray weight of the sky beyond the window. "One is that someone actually meant to kill your son — I'm sorry," he added, when Riley flinched at the suggestion. Jury took a sip of the whiskey under the approving eye of Beth Riley. Approving what? That the law drank on duty? Or that someone had meant to kill her stepson? "Another is that Simon might have known something that someone didn't want him to know. Seen something that someone hadn't wanted him to see. Simon could have had knowledge he didn't even *know* he had, too. The thing is that he was in an alley that none of his schoolmates seemed to know about. It's not on his way home from school. And school had been out over an hour, if the medical examiner fixed the time correctly. Somewhere between five and perhaps eight o'clock. It might make one think that someone had been, possibly, following him —"

Riley was into his third whiskey, drinking with blind eyes, the handkerchief wadded against his face. "He could have been dragged there —"

Jury was already shaking his head. "No. There'd be — signs, if that were the case." Bloodstains, marks — Jury didn't elaborate.

The Rileys exchanged glances, but shook their heads.

"Could he have been meeting someone?"

They looked blank.

"Kids get up to things —"

Riley was out of his chair like a shot. Wasn't it enough the boy was dead? Did police have to go about ruining his character, too? Even Beth got in on this scene. She mightn't have missed Simon, but the family name was something else again.

Jury rose and apologized for intruding upon them, as he took another look at the pictures, the memorabilia over the fireplace. Beth as a young girl, Beth as a young woman. Nothing of Riley that he could see. Wiggins stood beside him, notebook clapped shut, pocketing his pen, taking out his lozenges.

February was hell this close to the sea. Dorchester was ten miles from it, but that was close enough for Wiggins.

They stopped outside and Jury lit a cigarette. "We wouldn't have got any more out of them. And the boy's funeral is tomorrow. Leave it for now."

The queue of shoppers had disappeared, but Jury saw in the faces of passersby more fear than curiosity. They walked at the edge of the pavement, as if coming nearer the scene of such a tragedy might contaminate them, might spread danger to their own children.

The Closed sign hung a little askew. Wiggins was studying a brace of pheasant, feet trussed up, heads dangling down. "No need to cause more suffering." Jury thought he was referring to the Rileys, until he added, "That's why I've been thinking of going vegetarian."

Jury tried to drag his mind from the man whose son was dead and the son himself, to say, "No more plaice and chips, Wiggins? Hard to imagine."

Wiggins considered. "I think I'd still eat fish. But not flesh, sir."

"No more missionaries, that it?"

"Pardon?"

"Never mind." Jury smiled bleakly. "There's Judge Jeffries restaurant just down the road. You hungry? Nothing like eating under the eye of the Hanging Judge." Jury looked at the pheasant.

Man, beast, bird. Life is cheap.

II

And he knew just how cheap when they got back to Wynfield, where the Dorset police had its headquarters.

"There's been another one," said Inspector Neal, looking a little grayer than when Jury had last seen him. "In Wynchcoombe. Another boy: name, Davey White. Choirboy." Neal's voice broke and he did not look at all pleased that his theory was probably being proved correct. At the same time he looked slightly relieved, and guilty for the relief. "Not ours, though. This is the Devon-Cornwall constabulary's manor. Wynchcoombe's in Dartmoor." He was interrupted by the telephone — a call, apparently, from his superior, for he kept nodding. "Yes, yes, yes. We've got every man on it we can spare . . . yes, I *know* the town's in a panic . . ." After more from the other end, Neal hung up, shaking his head.

Jury said nothing except, "How far's Wynchcoombe, then?"

Neal looked a little surprised. "Forty miles, about."

A police constable — a pleasant-looking young man — showed Jury the map on the wall. "You'll want to go to headquarters first, I expect. That's just outside Exeter —"

"Why do I want to go there? What's the quickest way to Wynchcoombe?"

"Well, I was just thinking you'd want to check with headquarters. Sir," he added weakly.

"It'd only waste time."

Neal was making a fuss over some papers on his desk seemingly in desperate need of rearrangement. "That's Divisional Commander Macalvie's patch, Mr. Jury."

"I don't much care if it's Dirty Harry Callahan's. We've got a boy murdered in Dorchester and now another one in Wynchcoombe. So I'd like to get there as soon as possible. The divisional commander will understand."

The constable just looked at Jury. Then he said, "I worked with him once. Right cock-up I made of something and —" He pulled back the corners of his mouth. In a distorted voice he said, "I loss ta teeth. Crowns, these are."

Jury picked up the map the constable had marked the route on as Wiggins leaned closer and peered at his teeth. "I only wish I had your dentist."

II

The Church
in the Moor

THREE

THE silver chalice lay on the floor of the choir vestry, staining it darker with the wine that had been mixed with water now mixed with blood. Before the Scene of Crimes man had come, no one could touch it. After he had finished with it, no one wanted to. The lab crew of the Devon-Cornwall constabulary seemed to be avoiding it, superstitiously. As for the pictures, the police photographer had apologized to the curate for the little bursts of light in Wynchcoombe Church.

Police, both uniformed branch and CID, were all over the church, searching the chancel aisles, the nave, the main vestry. Wiggins and several others were outside going over the Green, on which the church fronted, and the deserted church walk, leading to the vestry doors on the other side.

Dr. Sanford, the local practitioner, had finished up his examination and said the boy had probably been dead around ten hours. The curate couldn't believe that the boy could have been there all that time and no one found him until three or four hours ago.

It had surprised Jury, too, who was standing down by the altar with TDC Coogan. He looked up at the altar, his mind a blank. Wynchcoombe had a beautiful church here. Even with its high spire, it appeared smaller on the outside than inside. The chancel and nave together measured over a hundred feet.

He could think of nothing to say to Betty Coogan, who was crying. She couldn't help herself, she said; she'd known Davey and his granddad, the vicar of Wynchcoombe Church. "Whoever'd want to do this to Davey White?"

In any other circumstances, Policewoman Coogan would have been a gift with her red hair and good legs. But not now.

It was the expression on the clear face of Davey White that had struck Jury most — a look not of terror but more of impish surprise, the mouth slightly open, smiling even, as if he'd thought it had been rather a wizard trick, this being struck without warning. Now here he lay, ten years old, another schoolboy, dead two days after Simon Riley.

Betty Coogan was talking about the boy in Dorchester, blowing her nose with Jury's handkerchief, voicing the opinion of the Dorset police: they had a psychopathic killer on their hands. Jury was more inclined to agree than he had been before, but he still withheld judgment. The method was the same. Simple. A knife in the back.

The fingerprint man came up to Jury and Coogan. "Where in hell's Macalvie?"

She shook her head, another bout of tears threatening. "In Exeter, on that robbery case. I tried to get him. Well, they must have got him by now —"

The print expert mumbled. "Ought to be here —"

He was. Divisional Commander — or Detective Chief Superintendent — Brian Macalvie came through the heavy oak doors of Wynchcoombe Church like the icy Dartmoor wind he brought with him. And he didn't tiptoe down the aisle.

The look he gave his TDC Betty Coogan did nothing at all to steady her. She seemed to sway a little, and Jury put his hand under her arm.

Chief Superintendent Macalvie looked briefly up at the altar and slightingly at them and said to Jury, "Who the hell are you?"

Jury took out his warrant card; Macalvie glanced at it and then at TDC Coogan (having dismissed Jury and all the credentials that went with him), saying, "You knew where I was. Why the bloody hell didn't you get to me sooner?"

She simply lowered her head.

"Where're you hiding the body, Betts? Might I have a wee look?"

There was a Scot's burr, probably put-on when he felt like it. Macalvie's accent seemed to have got stuck somewhere in the mid-Atlantic. But the Scotch ancestry reigned at the moment: accent, coppery hair, blue eyes like tiny blowtorches. Jury could understand why Betty Coogan didn't snap back.

Still with head lowered, she said, "He's in the choir vestry."

Macalvie stood in the vestry, still with hands jammed in trouser pockets, holding back his raincoat — which was the way he had come in. "By now, fifty percent of anything I could use has washed down the Dart." It sounded as if he were privy to some invisible world of evidence from which mere, mortal cops (the Jurys of the world) were excluded. Macalvie had been standing and looking down at the body, looking round the vestry, looking out the vestry door. He was standing now at the door, still with his hands in his pockets, just like anyone who might have been speculating on a sudden change of weather.

To his back, a CID sergeant named Kendall said, "Nothing's been touched, sir. Except for Dr. Sanford's examination of the body."

"That's like saying an archaeologist left the digs as neat as my gran's front parlor," said Macalvie to the mist and the vestry walk lost in it.

Jury saw Dr. Sanford look at Macalvie with a wild sort of anger — at the man standing there communing with the trees. The doctor opened his mouth, but shut it again.

Constable Coogan, cheeks burning, decided to fight fire. "You'd think anyone else just *looking* at the crime scene before you got there erases clues:—"

Macalvie turned those blowtorch eyes on her. "It does."

He nodded at the chalice. "What's that doing in the choir vestry?" Macalvie was down on one knee now, looking at the body of Davey White.

Dr. Sanford was an avuncular man who must have had an extensive National Health list of patients, as Wynchcoombe was an extensive parish. His smile — his first mistake — was condescending: "I assure you, Chief Superintendent, that the boy *wasn't* brained with the chalice. He was stabbed."

Macalvie favored Dr. Sanford with the same look he'd shot at TDC Coogan. "I didn't say he *was* 'brained', did I? I'm a simple, literal man. I asked a simple, literal question." He turned back to the body.

No one answered his question, so Dr. Sanford filled in the silence. "He's been dead, I'd judge, since about six o'clock this morning. Of course —"

"It could have been earlier or later." Macalvie finished the comment for him. "Not even you can tell the exact time of death. Not even me."

Dr. Sanford controlled himself and went on: "There's rigor, but the lividity —"

"You think it's hypostasis."

"Of course." Sanford continued his discourse on the blood's having drained and the darker patches of skin showing where the body had been in contact with the floor.

Macalvie, still with his eyes on Davey White's body, held out his hand as if he weren't paying any more attention to Sanford than a pew or a prayer-cushion. "Give me your scalpel."

Dr. Sanford was clearly shocked; his tone was frosty: "And did you intend to perform the autopsy here and now? You *do* have a pathologist —" He stopped and looked extremely uneasy. He might just as well not have been there at all, given the lack of response. Still, the doctor plowed the furrow: "I really don't think —"

Macalvie's hand was still outstretched. Jury imagined that when Macalvie was thinking himself, he didn't want those thoughts lost in the crossfire of underlings — TDCs, doctors, or even Scotland Yard.

Dr. Sanford reopened his bag and produced a scalpel.

Macalvie made a tiny incision in the center of one of the purplish stains and a bit of blood oozed and trickled. He returned the scalpel, pulled down the boy's vest, and said nothing.

Again, as if it were necessary to fill up silences Macalvie left in his wake, Sergeant Kendall said, "The curate couldn't understand how the lad could have been lying here for all that time —"

"Because the kid *wasn't* lying here all that time. That's a bruise, not hypostasis." He ignored Sanford and addressed himself to Jury, figuring, perhaps, since one nitwit had got it wrong, he wanted to hear if the other one would. It was the second time he'd spoken to Jury; Wiggins, he'd managed to neglect altogether. "What do you think?"

"I think you're right," said Jury. "He probably wasn't killed here and certainly hasn't been lying here for ten hours."

Macalvie continued to stare at Jury, but said nothing. Then he turned to his fingerprint man and indicated the silver chalice that had been carefully dusted and photographed. "You through with that?"

"Sir." He nearly clicked his heels and handed over the chalice.

In spite of its already having had a thorough going-over,

Macalvie handled it with a handkerchief, holding it up to the light as if he were administering the sacraments.

Betty Coogan, completely unnerved by her divisional commander and (Jury supposed) sometime-lover, asked, "You think he was killed somewhere else and brought here? But why? That doesn't make sense."

"Really?" said Macalvie in his loquacious way.

Jury shook his head. "That's taking a hell of a chance, unless the murderer was making a point. The chalice wouldn't be in the choir vestry except for someone's wanting to smear it in the boy's blood. An act of desecration."

Macalvie nearly forgot himself and smiled. "Okay, let's go and have a talk with his dad."

"Grandfather. Davey's own father is dead," said Wiggins, sliding a cough drop into his mouth.

"Okay, grandfather." Macalvie held out his hand as he had for the doctor's scalpel. "Mind giving me one of those? I'm trying to quit smoking."

"Good," said Wiggins, promptly letting a few Fisherman's Friends drop into Macalvie's palm. "You won't regret it."

II

Although the housekeeper was weeping when she opened the door, the Reverend Linley White's eyes were as dry as his voice.

Wiggins had been dispatched to get what he could out of the housekeeper (which, if nothing else, would be a cup of tea), and Jury and Macalvie were seated in two ladderback chairs on the other side of Mr. White's large desk. Even with one less policeman in the room, the vicar appeared to think the ratio of two to one was unfair, though God was supposedly his ally. He could tell them absolutely nothing that would throw light on this "sad affair" — a favorite summing up, apparently; he used it several times.

"Sure, you can throw some light on things," said Macalvie, pleasantly. "Such as why you didn't like him."

The vicar was vehement in his denial of this charge, especially coming, as it did, before he could find a persona to fit it. "David has been living here for just a little over a year. My son and his wife, Mary" — the *Mary* called up someone he'd sooner forget, apparently —"died in a motorcycle accident and shortly after that, her aunt simply dropped David — quite literally — on my doorstep. It was supposed to be for a few days. I've not laid eyes on the woman since. I don't know why I was surprised." Under a gray cliff of eyebrow, the vicar's eyes burned with un-Christian-like feeling.

Jury wondered if, in the vicar's fight against feeling for Mary, he had won the battle but lost the war. The Reverend White could — as he went on to do — call Davey's mother "pig-track Irish," but Jury saw the tattered flag of emotion in all of this, and thought it probably sexual.

Macalvie said, "So you didn't like Mary. Either."

"Now listen, Superintendent —"

"Chief." It must have been almost unconscious. Malcalvie wasn't even looking at White; his eyes were raking over the room as they had been doing ever since he sat down.

"*Chief* Superintendent. This has been one of the worst experiences of my life."

Macalvie looked at him then. "What was the other one?"

"Pardon?"

"It must have been pretty bad if your grandson's murder is only one of them. I can't believe there were more than two. So what I gather is, since you hated the mother, you didn't much care for sight of Davey around the house. Constant reminder, right?" He had just stuck a Fisherman's Friend in his mouth and was sucking at it.

Color drained from the vicar's face until it matched the shade of the bisque statuette on his desk. "*Certainly* I was fond of David. What are you trying to say?"

"I never *try* to say anything. I just say it. So was his mother the only reason you didn't like Davey?"

The vicar was half out of his chair now. "You persist in this judgment —"

"Judgments I leave up to God. Sit down. He was killed sometime early this morning. Five, six. Why would he have been out at that hour and in Wynchcoombe Wood?"

Mr. White was astonished. "But he was killed in the *church!*"

Macalvie shook his head. "He was *put* in the church. Probably at that hour there was nobody about. And barely light. But would no one have been in the church this morning? A char? Anyone?"

The vicar shook his head. "Not necessarily. And no reason for anyone to go into the choir vestry."

"You don't keep a very sharp eye on your grandson, do you?"

Jury interrupted, much to Macalvie's displeasure. "Why would Davey have been out that early?"

Mr. White colored, smarting still under the bite of Macalvie's comment, probably, Jury thought, because it was true.

"Davey was a bit odd —"

Macalvie's impatient sigh told him how much he believed that excuse.

"I *only* mean that he occasionally liked to get out of the house before breakfast, before school, and go to the woods to, as he said, just 'think about things.' He hadn't many school chums . . ." The vicar's voice trailed away under Macalvie's blue gaze.

Jury was himself thinking about Simon Riley. "Thinking about things" could have meant smoking the odd cigarette. Or just getting away. Another lonely boy, perhaps, in a cold house. But he didn't voice his opinion.

Macalvie did. "Must have had a great life, your Davey. Didn't you worry about him, out in the dark or the dawn, alone in the wood?" He had got up to prowl the room and was now looking over the vicar's bookcases.

"Nothing's ever happened in Wynchcoombe Wood."

Macalvie raised his eyes from an old volume. "Something has now. And didn't you read about that kid in Dorchester, Mr. White?" he asked casually.

For the first time, the Reverend Linley White looked frightened. "I did. You're not saying there's a psychopathic killer loose?"

Macalvie's answer was another question. "Can you think of anyone who hated your grandson?"

"No. Absolutely not," he snapped.

"How about someone who might hate you?"

This time, the vicar had to stop and think.

III

What Wiggins had learned from the housekeeper verified the information they had got from the vicar. Except the house-keeper did wonder why Davey hadn't come back for his breakfast and his schoolbooks. Wiggins read his notes, and they were, as usual, thorough. Jury told him to go along to Wynchcoombe Wood. Macalvie cadged a few Fisherman's Friends and told Wiggins he wanted Kendall and his men to comb that vestry walk inch-by-inch. Davey could have stumbled, fallen, been dragged. That might account for the bruises.

Wiggins put away his notebook. "Yes, sir. You having an incidents room set up, sir?"

His yes was grudging. "Tell Kendall to get a portable unit and stick it in the middle of the damned Green." He nodded toward the clutch of villagers standing in front of the George and the tea room. Even from this distance, they seemed to pull back a bit, as if from fear, or, perhaps, the divisional commander's eye. "No, Wiggins," said Macalvie wearily, as

the sergeant wrote it down. "Put it in that parking lot —"
Macalvie nodded off to the right and a large lot, probably
meant for the cars and caravans of summer tourists. "And tell
Kendall to keep it staffed with the few men from headquarters who won't be stumbling all over their own feet. Much
less mine."

The church had been cordoned off; now, perhaps to disen-
gage themselves from the scene of the tragedy (or from Macalvie's stare), several of the villagers repaired to the pub,
there to overhaul their former estimate of life in sleepy little
Wynchcoombe.

"Pretty place," said Macalvie, qualifying it with, "if you
like this sort of village."

It was indeed a pretty place, with its stone cottages huddled around the Green and the spire of Wynchcoombe
Church rising above it. An enviable peal of bells told them it
was six.

"I need a drink," said Macalvie.

"The George?" Its sign claimed it to be a fourteenth-cen-
tury coaching inn.

He grunted. "You kidding? With all the regulars in there
having a crack about what happened? There's a pub a couple
miles away I go to when I feel especially masochistic. How
Freddie — you'll love Freddie — gets any custom on that
stretch of road beats me."

Macalvie looked off across a ground mist just beginning to
rise. "It's not far from a village called Clerihew Marsh. I
want to tell you a story, Jury."

FOUR

H ELP the Poor Struggler was the pub's full name, a wretched box of a building on a desolate stretch of road, whose ocher paint had dulled to the color of bracken from the smoke of its chimney pots. Its sign swung on an iron post over its door and the windows were so dirty they were opaque. The building listed from either dry rot or rising damp. Only the desolation of pub and traveler alike would tempt one to join the other.

There was no car park. What custom the pub got had to pull up by the side of the road. Two cars were there when Macalvie and Jury pulled in.

Brian Macalvie was now pursuing, with what Jury supposed was the customary Macalvie charm, a line of questioning directed at an arthritic, elderly woman who was swabbing down the bar. The "saloon" side was separated from the "public" side only by gentlemen's agreement. The public bar off to the left had most of the action: pool table, video game, Art Deco jukebox that was pummeling the customers with Elvis Presley's "Hound Dog."

* * *

"Where's Sam Waterhouse, Freddie?" Macalvie didn't so much ask for as demand an answer.

"I don't naw nort," said Freddie. "Y'm mazed as a brish stick, Mac. D'yuh niver quit?" She was wall-eyed, wattle-armed, and skinny, and with her stubby gray hair sitting in a lick on her head, she reminded Jury even more of a rooster. He guessed her sexual identity had been scratching with the chickens long enough to get lost.

"I never quit, Freddie. You treated Sam like you were his auld mum, the dear Lord help him."

"Ha! Yu'm a get vule, Mac, the divil hisself. Cider hisses when yu zwallers it."

"Hell, *this* cider'd hiss on a stone. You're thick as two boards and your right hand hasn't seen your left in forty years," said Macalvie, picking up his cider and moving to a table.

Freddie grinned at Jury. "What c'n I do ver 'ee, me anzum?"

Jury grinned back. "I'll try the cider. You're only young once."

"It was the stupidist arrest the Devon-Cornwall cops ever made." Macalvie was talking about the Rose Mulvanney case. "Here's this nineteen-year-old kid, Sam, who's living in Clerihew Marsh and indulging in fantasies, maybe about Cozy Rosie. Rose Mulvanney could start breathing heavy over anything in pants. In the U.S. she'd freak out in a corn-field over the scarecrows."

From what Macalvie had told Jury during their drive to the pub, it was certain the divisional commander's heart was in America — his mother was Irish-American — even if his body was in Devon. Obsessive as he was about police work, still he took his vacation every year and went to New York. His speech was littered with the old-fashioned, hard-boiled speech of a Bogart movie: *dames, broads*—that sort of thing.

"How do you know all this stuff about Rose Mulvanney?"

"Through extremely delicate questions put to the inhabitants of Clerihew Marsh," said Macalvie. "Like, did Rose screw around—"

"I'm sure that's the way you put it." Jury took a drink of cider and could believe in the sizzling throat of the devil.

"Be careful, Freddie makes it herself. My questions to the villagers were more disgustingly discreet. But what turned up when I collared the milkman and the old broad that runs the post office stores was that Rose Mulvanney, a couple of days before she died, started taking more milk and buying more bread. *This* even though her kid Mary was away on a school trip. The extra groceries went on for maybe five days. Now, she sure as hell wasn't doing that for Sammy Waterhouse. He lived right there in Clerihew Marsh."

"You're saying someone else was living with her?"

"Of course."

Jury tried not to smile. Macalvie was nothing if not certain of Macalvie. "I agree it's a possibility."

"Good. I can go on living." He popped another Fisherman's Friend into his mouth.

"So, assuming the Devon-Cornwall police picked on Waterhouse — why? Months went by before they arrested him, you said."

"It's expensive to mount a murder investigation; you know that. They wanted to get him a hell of a lot earlier, except I kept tossing spanners in the works, like trying to convince the effing Devon police that Sam Waterhouse couldn't have moved in with Rose."

"Aren't you making a lot out of extra bread and milk?"

"No. Rose wasn't buying bread for the church bazaar."

"There must have been evidence against Waterhouse. What was it?"

"That he was always mooning around Rose. He was *nineteen*, for God's sakes." Macalvie shoved the ashtray to the end of the table. "And the dame next door said she'd heard them having a king-sized row a few nights before Rose died. She saw Sam coming out of the house in a right blaze."

"And Waterhouse — what did he say?"

"He didn't deny it. He was furious Rose had been 'leading him on' and he really thought she cared. Told him she had another boyfriend, stuff like that."

"What did forensics turn up?"

"Their hands. They just shrugged. Of *course* there were prints. All over. Sam had admitted to being in the house. But on the knife? No. He'd have wiped that clean, said my learned superior. So I said to him, Then why didn't he wipe everything *else* clean he'd touched? And after the elimination prints — the two daughters and a couple of friends in Clerihew — there were still two sets left over. Could have been anybody, and certainly could have been the guy who did the job, if he'd been living there for a few days."

"The girls? The daughters? Where were they?"

"The fifteen-year-old was off on a school trip. The little one must have been in the house, except for the odd night or two she was sent to play with a little chum from her school."

"But that means she must have seen the man at some point — assuming you're right."

Macalvie's look sliced up Jury as good as any knife. Could there be any doubt about a Macalvie theory? "That's true. All she had to do was say, 'No, it wasn't Sammy.' And believe me, she would have if she could; she was crazy about Sam. Both girls were. He was very nice to them. So she could have said it wasn't him and maybe identify who it *was*. Only Teresa never spoke another word." Macalvie turned to stare into the inglenook fireplace, as if he too might never speak another word, a rare silence for him, Jury thought.

In the public bar off to the left, Freddie had muscled an anti-Elvis fan away from the jukebox to feed in her own coins. "Jailhouse Rock" made way for "Are You Lonesome Tonight?"

Jury saw Macalvie glance toward the jukebox and thought perhaps he was going to answer the question put by Elvis — and, for that matter, by Freddie, who was singing along: "D'ya miss me tooo-night?" in her cups and out of key. Macalvie snatched up both of their pints, saying, "It wouldn't be so bloody bad if Freddie'd shut up." He walked over to the bar, had his brief quarrel with her — their standard means of communication, Jury imagined — and was back and picking up the story of the Mulvanney family. He chronicled their lives as if he'd been a relation. The details he'd picked up during the investigation.

"It still seems like pretty shabby evidence," said Jury.

Macalvie drank his cider. "Oh, of course the prosecution had their witness. No, not someone who saw it. Just a friend of Sammy's."

"Friend? Doesn't sound like much of one."

"Ah, but in the interests of Justice, we must all do our bit. He was a student at Exeter, too. Law. Claimed Sam Waterhouse had said several times he'd kill her. Good old George, standing right there in the box saying Sam came in that night with what looked like blood on his clothes. Liar."

"What was Waterhouse's answer?"

"That if he ever said it, it was only a manner of speaking. And the blood came from cutting himself in the lab. Terrific. The prosecution made mincemeat of Sam."

Whether from the aftereffects of cider or the present effects of Elvis, Freddie was still singing along:

> *"Doon yer haaaart fill wit pain?*
> *Should ay COME beck a-GAAAIIN? . . ."*

wailed Freddie. Macalvie yelled at her to shut up. Freddie paid no attention.

"Christ, an Elvis song that doesn't bring down the walls and she's got to have a sing-along. The kid, Mary Mulvanney," Macalvie went on, "I saw her twice. Once at the inquest. She could hardly answer the questions."

He stopped, stared at the jukebox, then back at Jury.

"Unfortunately, I wasn't there. I wasn't in charge of the case. Bad luck for Devon. What I did, I did on my own. Didn't amount to much. A few questions here, a few bruises there." His blue eyes glinted with reflected firelight and he almost smiled. "That's supposed to be my style, you know. Threats, blackmail, bullets in knee-caps." He shrugged.

"I don't worry too much about style. When was the second time?"

Macalvie was staring into the fire again, shoving his foot against one of the huge logs sprawled on the hearth like an old dog. "For what?"

Jury knew Macalvie knew "for what." "The second time you saw Mary Mulvanney."

"Months later. After they tossed Sam Waterhouse in the nick. The kid storms in my office — fifteen, scrawny, and freckles — talk about scarecrows. But, man, did she let me have it. She knew some words even I didn't know; must have been some swell school she was going to. I never saw anyone so mad in my life."

"Why at you? You were the one person who kept the case open and did all the work."

"So to her that meant I was in charge, didn't it? She knew Waterhouse didn't do it. And she screamed at me, as she casually removed all the stuff from my desk with a delicate sweep of her skinny arm: *That's my mum got killed and my baby sister's in hospital and you'd fucking well better get who did it or I will!'* My God, could that kid get mad."

But Macalvie, who had seemed determined not to temper bad humor with good, was actually smiling. It was probably a relief to him to find somebody who wasn't afraid of him, even if she was only a skinny young kid.

"And then she stormed out. I never saw her again." The

look he gave Jury was woeful. "It was the only case I never solved."

He wanted Jury to think that was the source of the unhappy look. Jury didn't.

II

They had been sitting there for a couple of minutes, in a small pocket of silence not shared by the regulars who were being treated to the wonderful voice of Loretta Lynn. Unfortunately, the coalminer's daughter had to make way to the voice-over of Freddie, behind the bar wiping glasses and singing about how she too once had to go to the well to draw water.

Macalvie yelled at her, "The last time you ever drank anything but booze was when they tossed you in Cranmere Bog."

"What about the little one, Teresa?"

"What about her?"

"If you're right —"

Raised eyebrows. *If?*

"Then why in hell did the killer leave a witness behind?"

That this could be a hole in his theory did not seem to bother Macalvie at all. He could, apparently, plug it up like a finger in a dike. "Say because the guy was sure Teresa couldn't tie him to her mother. Maybe Teresa *didn't* see him, or at least didn't know his name, or for a dozen reasons she simply wouldn't be able to point a finger at him. And if it were a crime of passion, it's possible that he couldn't see his way to killing a five-year-old, too."

"And the five-year-old? Could she have gone after her mum with a knife? Did you ever suspect her?"

The look Macalvie gave Jury could have carved him in pieces. "No, I always do thing by halves, Jury. I'm a sloppy cop. I didn't even notice the trail of blood she left all the way from the kitchen to the phone and all the blood over her nightie and on the phone —" He waved a dismissive hand. "Don't be an asshole, will you? Of course, little kids can wig out. She didn't do it." He was silent for a while. Then he said, "I went to the hospital. It was obvious, at least in the mumbo-jumbo land of shrinkdom, that she didn't stand much chance of getting well. Her mind seemed to have split. Catatonic and curled up like a fetus. Anyway, they finally moved Teresa to Harbrick Hall. Ever heard of it? They call it 'Heartbreak Hall.' "

Jury had heard of it. It was one of those places he wished he hadn't. "I was there once."

"And you're almost cured?"

Jury ignored the sarcasm, thinking of Harbrick Hall. One of those cozy, innocent-sounding names that in no way reflected its huge, understaffed, overfull hospital. Endless corridors, bolted doors, grilles. The sickly, sour smell of urine and ammonia, and the gray-garbed janitor with mop and pail in a corridor awash in hopelessness.

Macalvie went on: "The place is so big you could get lost just trying to find your way out. Anyway, Teresa Mulvanney supposedly had got a little better. No, she wasn't talking. She never talked. But at least she wasn't lying curled up like a baby. The Paki attendant 'very proud' of Teresa's 'progress.' Progress. You know what her progress was?"

From Macalvie's tone, Jury didn't think he wanted to know. Right now, he couldn't get the faces of Simon Riley and Davy White out of his mind. They seemed to merge and separate and break apart, like little faces behind mullioned and rained-on windowpanes.

"Fingerpainting," said Macalvie. "The Paki couldn't understand why 'she only like the red pot.' "

"Drop it." He blotted out the image of fingerpaints by trying to concentrate on the Irish singer someone had mercifully found on the jukebox. Jury was sure his display of weakness would earn him a surly answer.

But all Macalvie said was, "I did." He looked at his watch. "But Mary, the sister, couldn't, could she?" He turned to look at the jukebox from which came the lovely and mournful dirge:

> *I love you as I never loved before,*
> *Since first I met you on the village green . . .*

Macalvie was taking money out of his wallet and was out of his chair as quick as a cat. In one long movement, he tossed the money on the table of the man who'd slotted the ten p in the box and then he walked over and pulled the plug before the singer could finish *"as I loved you, when . . ."*

Freddie tossed down her bar-towel and started over; the man who'd played the song was bigger than Macalvie and getting out of his chair. Knowing that Macalvie — outsized, outweighed, or outnumbered — wouldn't hesitate to shove the man right back down again, Jury started to get up. Damned idiot. Couldn't he remember he was a cop?

Apparently, he could. The jukebox was in the public bar and so were Macalvie and his newfound friends; Jury couldn't hear what he said, but Macalvie was shoving his wallet in the big one's face and smiling. Freddie was standing with her hands on her skinny hips. The party at the table got their coats together pretty quickly, and Macalvie turned to Freddie, who gave him a bar-towel in the face.

At least that pleased the regulars who were on their way out. Macalvie just shrugged and came back to sit down.

"Pulling rank? That could be dangerous down at headquarters," said Jury.

That earned him an uncomprehending stare. Dangerous for Macalvie? "I don't pull rank, buddy." His elbow on the table, he turned his watch so Jury could see it. "You never heard of the licensing laws? I just told them Freddie had to close early and asked if anyone was in a condition to drive, seeing all the cider they'd put down." He picked up his and

Jury's pints and strolled across the pub, which they now had to themselves."

Except, of course, for Freddie, who was filling the pints and Macalvie's ear with her opinion of him. It followed him across the room, silenced only by his turning and saying — Elvis done with, he didn't have to yell — "I'd of run you into Princetown years ago, Freddie, except I've got a certain respect for the murderers and psychos there."

He slammed down the pints, waterfalling the cider down the glasses as Freddie went to answer the telephone. "Christ, what a stupid old broad. That 'Freddie' doesn't stand for 'Frederika,' or any girl's name. Stands for 'Fred.' The mum and dad must've wanted a boy; they'd have settled for a girl; they got a mineral." He drank his cider.

"Telephone, me anzum," fluted Freddie.

"She must mean you, Jury. She'd never call me that."

It was Inspector Neal, who had tracked him down through Kendall. What he had to report about his end of the investigation was very little. But a Chief Superintendent Racer had called and asked — well, *demanded* was a better word — that Jury report to him. And how was he getting on with Divisional Commander Macalvie?

"Swell," said Jury. "Friendly guy."

"That's a first," said Neal, and hung up.

Jury went back to the table and started to collect his coat. "It's not that I don't enjoy sitting around with you, but we've got two murders on our hands."

"One's mine. Don't be greedy, Jury."

"One's yours. I'd never know it. You can sit here and drink the night away and yell at Freddie. I'm going back to Dorchester."

"Can you just sit down a minute and shut up. Do you think I'm relaxing in the Victorian splendor of this roach-ridden flashhouse because I want to? Why in hell do you think I've been talking about the Mulvanney murder?"

"Because you're obsessed with it, maybe?"

Macalvie didn't rise to the bait. "Because in my gut, I know there's a connection."

As Jury asked him what, the door of the Help the Poor Struggler opened and shut behind them.

"I think it just walked in."

He sounded sad.

FIVE

JURY would have recognized the prison pallor anywhere; he'd seen it often enough. It wasn't the pale skin of a man who'd not seen enough of the sun. It was more as if one had put a paintbrush to an emotion — despair, desolation, whatever — and tinged it in that sickly whitish-gray. The pallor was accentuated by the black clothes: chinos, roll-neck sweater, parka. Accentuated too by the dark hair and eyes. He was tall, understandably thin, handsome, and maybe in mourning for nineteen lost years.

"Hullo, Sam," said Macalvie.

"I wondered who the car belonged to. I should've known."

Freddie came out from some inner room as if her antennae had at last picked up a welcome presence. "Sammy!" She flung herself against him so hard that Jury was surprised he didn't hear bones breaking. She stepped back and gave Macalvie an evil look. Then to Sam, she said, "How are yuh, me dear?"

"I'm fine, Freddie. Just waiting for the place to clear."

Macalvie, who always knew what everyone else was thinking, smiled. "I know. I cleared it. So sit down, Sammy." With his foot, he shoved out a chair. And, as if they were on the best of terms, he said to her, "Freddie, bring the man some cider and go play Elvis. Just don't play 'Jailhouse Rock,' okay? Or I'll break your knees. Where've you been, Sam? You got out four days ago."

"You keeping track, Inspector? But it couldn't be inspector now. You must be chief constable."

"I will be. Right now it's commander. Or chief superintendent."

"Where'd you trip up?" asked Sam, as Freddie put down his pint. "Not over me, I hope." But his smile was hopeless.

"Who tripped up? You think I'm ambitious?"

Sam Waterhouse's laugh was so hearty that Freddie came out to check on things. She disappeared again.

"What've you been doing?"

"Seeing Dartmoor. Sleeping in an old tin-working or on the rocks. I like the moor. The way the mist comes up, the whole damned world disappears. Ever been up on Hound Tor? Nice. On a clear day you can see Exeter and police headquarters forever. Why don't you forget it, Macalvie?"

"Read any papers lately, Sam?"

Sam Waterhouse shifted uncomfortably in his chair and drank off nearly half of his pint. "Sure. The newsboy was flogging the *Telegraph* all over Dartmoor."

"Meaning you have," said Macalvie. "Meet any other tourists?"

Jury both could and couldn't understand Sam Waterhouse's anger. If you'd been in a high-security lockup on a trumped-up charge. Except Macalvie was the one who'd always believed in Sam's innocence and who'd worked like hell to prove it.

"I saw the papers. A boy was killed in Dorchester. What's it to do with me?"

"And another kid was killed in Wynchcoombe. You

wouldn't have read about that yet. Look. I'm not asking you for alibis."

"What are you asking for then?"

Macalvie shook his head. "Not sure."

Jury was surprised Macalvie could say it.

Sam Waterhouse took one of Jury's cigarettes. He had the hoarse voice of a heavy smoker. Jury didn't imagine nineteen years in Princetown would make a voice mellifluous.

"You're still trying to solve that case." Sam shook his head.

"It's a blot on my career." Macalvie's smile did its quick little disappearing act. "Incidentally, you're sitting next to a CID man from Scotland Yard."

"Richard Jury," said Jury, embellishing upon Macalvie's gracious introduction. He shook hands with Sam Waterhouse.

"You can't be working our mutual friend Macalvie's manor? It's mined."

"Jury's working on the Dorchester case. It just happened to spill over into Devon."

"Too bad. But neither of them has sod-all to do with me."

"Has anyone accused you of anything?"

"Where would I get that idea? I walk into Freddie's, and who do I find but you, lying in wait." He leaned closer. "Macalvie, doesn't it occur to you that I want to *forget* about Rose Mulvanney?"

"It had crossed my mind. That 'other boyfriend' she had —"

"I don't want to talk about it."

"She never mentioned any names?"

Sam Waterhouse closed his eyes in pain. "Don't you think I'd have damned well *said* if I knew of anyone else? I looked at her diary; I went through her desk. All that got me was a shadowy snapshot of some man. I asked her who it was and she said her uncle." Sam shrugged.

"Well, we didn't find anything like that. Uncle must have taken diary, photos, and papers."

Sam's eyes glittered with anger. "Look, all of this has been said and said again." His face took on the look of the chronic loser. "For God's sakes, haven't you had any murders in Devon in the last nineteen years so you want to hook these up with the Mulvanney case?" Macalvie shook his head. "Then why here and why now?"

"Revenge, Sam. At least, that's what the papers —"

Sam Waterhouse shook his head. "I don't know what you're talking about. You've got a psychopath on your hands —"

"I don't think so. At least not in the sense you mean — that there's no connection between the kids' murders."

Freddie stomped in with a steaming plate of mutton, boiled potatoes and vegetables. She plunked it down in front of Sam and gave Macalvie an evil look as if he'd been the prison cook. Sam went at the food with a vengeance.

Macalvie went on: "You've been out walking the moor for four days? Why?"

"Because I've been in the nick for nineteen years and wanted to see a little open space. As soon as I'm finished with this meal, you can slap the cuffs on me. I'll go quietly, Commander."

"Well, arresting you's not what I had in mind. You staying here?"

"Probably. Freddie's been like a mother to me."

Macalvie feigned surprise. "A mother? She's not even female. What I was really waiting for was to talk to you. You could be helpful."

Waterhouse leaned back in his chair and laughed: it was a transforming laugh; Jury could see in his face the nineteen-year-old student of medicine. "Help the Devon-Cornwall constabulary? I think I'd go back to Princetown first." That incandescent look of youth fell away like a falling star. "Even if I *would* 'help,' I couldn't. I don't know any more now than I did then. And I didn't know anything then."

"How do you know?"

Sam looked up from his plate. "Meaning what?"

"You might know something that you didn't connect with Rose's murder, or you might know something you don't know —"

"I had nineteen years to think it over. Case closed."

"Let's say I just reopened it."

III

The Marine Parade

SIX

Angela Thorne had been told by her parents never to stay out after dark, never to miss her tea, never to walk along the Cobb, never to play along the shingle beach when the tide was coming in. Angela Thorne was presently engaged in doing them all, attended only by her dog, Mickey.

Dark had come by five o'clock, and she was still out in it two hours later. Some of that time had been spent wandering aimlessly in the well-tended gardens above the Marine Parade. A further half-hour she'd spent going up and down several little flights of steps along the Parade and moving backward toward the stone wall to beat the running tide.

She was presently breaking another injunction by walking along the dark arm of the Cobb that made a safe harbor for the little fishing boats, creaking out there in the wind and the water.

Mickey puffed along behind her. He was a terrier and too fat because Angela kept feeding him scraps of food from her plate, disgusting things like mashed swede or blood pudding or skate that always looked to her like the clipped wing of some big bird. All Mickey was supposed to eat was dried dog food. He was old, and her parents were afraid he'd have a heart attack.

She was tired of her parents and she hated her school. She hated nearly everything. Probably, it was because she wasn't pretty, and having to wear this long braid and hard shells of glasses. No one else at school had to wear thick glasses. Her classmates teased her constantly.

Angela stopped far out on the Cobb to look back at the lights of Lyme Regis along the Marine Parade. She had never seen Lyme at night from this distance. She liked that un-earthly glow of the lamps. The little town seemed light-lifted above the black sea.

She wished it would fall in and drown. Angela didn't like Lyme, either.

The tattoo of Mickey's paws scraping stone continued as Angela walked on. Mickey loved the sea. When the tide was out, he'd tear away from her like a bit of white cloth in the wind and chase the ruffs of waves as if he'd never felt free-dom before, as if he were having the time of his life.

II

She took off her cape and threw it over the little girl. Better to freeze than have to look at the blood-soaked dress of the body on the black rocks. The small dog was hysterical — running to nose at the cape, then back to Molly, going dog-crazy.

Standing on the high-piled rocks at the end of the Cobb, Molly Singer felt removed from the scene, a dream figure, looking down; a nonparticipant, the prying eye of some god.

In the seamless merging of sea and sky she could find no horizon. There was a chalky moon, and the sky was ham-mered with stars. And a distance off were the lights along the Parade.

Back and forth ran the dog. She would have to do something about the dog. Molly had a vision of the little girl and her dog, walking out along the Cobb, two dark silhouettes against the darker outline of the seawall.

She would have to get the dog back to shore. She was freezing, but at least she couldn't see the body now, which was the important thing.

Holding on to the dog, which struggled in her arms, she picked her way over the rocks and back to the seawall. On one of the dogtags was the name of its cottage.

She found Cobble Cottage and left the dog there, inside the gate.

Molly stood on the deserted Marine Parade, her own rented cottage at her back, the cold forgotten as she leaned against the railing where seaweed was tied like scarves, thrown up by the tide. The wooden groins along the shingle kept the sand from shifting. It would be nice if the mind could build itself such a protective wall.

She looked along the Cobb to the pile of rocks from which she had come.

All she could think of was the line from Jane Austen. *The young people were all wild to see Lyme.*

SEVEN

ELEVEN it might have been, but the manager of the White Lion didn't argue about the licensing laws any more than had Freddie's customers — though here it worked in reverse. The manager reopened the bar and smiled conspiratorially after Jury and Wiggins booked rooms. "Residents only," he said.

Wiggins, probably in some attempt to stay the awful effects of sea air, went straight to bed. It was the weather that had forced Jury and Wiggins to stop on the way back from Wynchcoombe. Rain and sleet that finally turned to hail. Each time a rock-sized chunk hit the windscreen, Wiggins veered. Jury imagined he was taking it personally, the weather. Weather and seasons were judged only in reference to Wiggins's health: spring brought allergies; autumn, a bleak prognosis of pneumonia; winter (the killer season), colds and fevers and flu. Driving along the Dorchester Road, Jury knew what was going on in his sergeant's mind, though mind-reading wasn't necessary: Wiggins was always pleased to open his Pandora's box of physical complaints and enlighten Jury as to which one had just flown by.

Before that could happen, Jury pointed out the turn to Lyme Regis.

Wiggins wasn't any too happy about sea-frets, either.

Jury got his pint, asked for the phone, and called headquarters in Wynchcoombe to let them know where he was. On his way back to the bar, he noticed a thin, elderly woman in a floppy hat watching a television as antiquated as she was.

Jury was slotting ten-p pieces into a stupid video game when she passed behind him, saying, "You can put money in that thing all night and you won't get any back. It's rigged." She went up to the bar and knocked on it with her knuckles for service.

"Thanks for the advice," said Jury, smiling. "Buy you a drink?"

"I wouldn't mind."

The manager, coming from an inner room, didn't seem surprised to see her.

"You a resident, then?" asked Jury.

"Off and on." She was wearing spectacles with sunglasses attached on tiny hinges. Why she needed the sunglasses in the murky light of the saloon bar, Jury couldn't imagine. She flipped them up and squinted at Jury as if he were light that hurt her eyes. "What's your name?"

"Richard Jury."

She snapped the brown-tinted glasses down again. "Hazel Wing," she said. The manager had already set up a pint of Guinness for Hazel Wing. Jury bought a drink for the manager, too.

Hazel Wing raised her glass and said, "Here's to getting through another one."

"Another what?" asked Jury.

"Day." Up went the sunglasses again and she squinted. This time, probably, to see if he was a little on the dim side.

"I'll drink to that, certainly."

"What do you do, if I may be so bold?"

"I'm a cop."

This news did not seem to surprise her. She said, "Oh. I sort of thought so."

"Why? Do I look like one?"

"No. You're better-looking. I just supposed it was about the little girl."

He felt himself go cold. "What do you mean?"

"That girl that's gone missing. Don't know her. Young. Got all of Lyme in a panic. You know. After that boy in Dorchester." Hazel Wing, who seemed the sort to chop off emotions as she did her sentences, still allowed herself a shudder. "Kids. Parents keeping them in. Dorchester's not far."

And neither was Wynchcoombe. "Excuse me." Jury put down his pint and made for the telephone again.

He stared in silence at the telephone in the lobby of the hotel. Constable Green, in the Lyme police station, had finally to ask if Jury had got the message. "Yes. Don't move her." He hung up while the constable was assuring him no one would touch her.

"Bad news," said Hazel Wing. It was a statement, not a question. News came only in one way to her.

"What's the quickest way to the Cobb Arms?"

"Walking or driving?"

"Whichever's faster."

Hazel Wing evaluated Jury's six-feet-two and decided, for him, walking. "Straight down the hill and right on the Marine Parade. That pub's at the other end. Ten minutes. If you're in a hurry."

"Thanks," he said.

"Good luck," she said, the words unconvincing. Luck, like news, was seldom good.

II

The little girl under the cape was lying as if she'd been stuffed like a small sack in the crevice of the rock.

"Hold the torch over here, will you?" Jury knelt down and picked the seaweed from her icy cheek. He knew he shouldn't have touched her at all before the doctor or Scene of Crimes expert got there, but he felt he had to get that stuff off her face. Bladder wrack. He remembered it from a seaside town he had gone to as a boy. It was the stuff that would pop if you squeezed it. A wave collapsed against the rocks, spewing foam in their faces. The wet rocks made standing difficult.

"Do you suppose she came out here," asked Constable Green on a hopeful note, "to get the dog and then was trapped by the waves. . . ?"

"No," said Jury. "It was a knife."

III

When Jury and Green got back to the Lyme Regis police station, Chief Superintendent Macalvie had been there for a quarter of an hour and ticking off every minute of it like a bomb.

Throughout Green's explanation of the anonymous telephone call and his finding the body, Macalvie sat in a chair tilted against the wall, sucking on a sourball. "So where's the body?"

"Hospital," said Green. "We got the local doctor —"

"Did he see her before she was moved?"

Green retreated into monosyllables. "Yes."

"About this woman, Molly Singer —" Macalvie was waiting for Green to embroider upon his description. Green didn't, so Macalvie went on. "Correct me if I'm wrong: you know the cape belongs to the Singer woman, you have a suspicion it was this woman who left the mutt at the Thornes' cottage, and you also suspect she was the one who rang up, and yet with all of this, you haven't brought her in for questioning."

"We went to her cottage, sir." Green looked from Jury to Macalvie, uncertain as to who had jurisdiction here: Dorset, Devon, or Scotland Yard? "But you don't know Molly Singer, sir —"

"Obviously I don't know her, Green. She isn't here, is she?" Macalvie looked around the room. Then he said to Wiggins, who had been dragged from under his eiderdown quilt around two A.M., "Give me one of those Fisherman's things, will you?"

Wiggins did so. He was presently trying to fend off something terminal, in a chair drawn up to a single-bar electric fire, where his feet competed with a large ginger cat snugly curled there.

Macalvie went on. "Because if she *was* here, then maybe the three of us could have a nice chin-wag and figure out what the hell she was doing on the end of the Cobb tonight."

Constable Green kept his expression as flat as the side of a slag heap and answered: "The Singer woman has lived in that cottage facing the Parade for nearly a year. No one in Lyme really knows her. She doesn't chat up the neighbors. She isn't friendly. She doesn't go out, except I've seen her sometimes at night, walking my beat. You might say she's eccentric —"

Jury interrupted. "You might say she's phobic, from what you told me earlier. Doesn't go out to the shops; doesn't mix with people at all . . ."

"I wouldn't know about that." Green turned to Jury with relief. "I've seen her a few times when I was making my rounds. I know that cape. Only, I couldn't make up an Identikit on her. That's how much she shows her face."

Macalvie's chair slammed down. "I don't believe it, Green. I just don't *believe* it — that a person you think could be a witness, could be even the chief suspect —"

"I never meant to say that." Green's voice rose in alarm. "It's just she won't talk to police."

Macalvie looked at Green and shook his head. He leaned across the PC's desk and his blue eyes sparked like matches. "We're talking murder, and all you can say is the chief witness is incommunicado." Macalvie got up. "Come on," he said to Jury, heading for the door. He looked over his shoulder at Wiggins, who had now grown as sluggish as the orange cat that had oozed its body straight out, paws fore and aft, stomach to glowing bar. That it was lying across the feet of Scotland Yard did not impress it at all.

"Wiggins," said Macalvie. "You going to toast crumpets or move?"

"You think the three of us are going to the Singer woman's house?" asked Jury.

"Of course."

"Kick in the door? Is that it?" Jury was putting his coat on. Macalvie had never taken his off. "Try to browbeat someone who's agoraphobic and see how far you get, Macalvie. I'll go by myself, thanks. This is Dorset, remember? Not your patch; at the moment, it's mine."

Macalvie was still sucking on the Fisherman's Friend. "Pulling rank. Well. And would you mind if I went out on my own and had a word with the Thornes? The dad and mum? And as long as you're going on your own, can I borrow your sergeant?"

He didn't wait for permission. The door of the station slammed after Macalvie and Wiggins.

EIGHT

Jury's idea of eccentricity might have been Hazel Wing. It wasn't Molly Singer, in spite of her off-the-rack Oxfam clothes: a shapeless sweater, a long and equally shapeless skirt. Jury guessed she was in her thirties; he had expected someone much older.

The fire and a napping cat were the only things that gave the room a semblance of warmth. It was a typical holiday cottage, furnished with remnants that could have been washed up from a shipwreck — mismatched sling chairs, a small cabinet whose open shelf held several bottles of liquor, a lumpyish love seat now occupied by the cat. In front of the window was an all-purpose table. Nothing here but the bare essentials.

Probably she was following the drift of his thoughts. "In the summer, this place costs the earth. It's right on the Parade, has an ocean view, and the landlord cleans up."

"I can imagine," said Jury.

"I even had to buy the lamp —" She nodded toward a small, blue-shaped lamp, useless for reading or anything but giving off a watery light. "I hope you don't mind the dark. I'm used to it by now."

Jury looked down at some books of poetry on the table and wondered if there was a double meaning in the comment. Emily Dickinson. Robert Lowell.

"You like poetry? I've always liked those lines of Lowell: 'The light at the end of the tunnel / Is the light of an oncoming train.'" She seemed to be talking out of sheer nervousness. "You could say I rent the cat, too. It wanders in every day and takes the best seat." The cat could have been mistaken for a black pillow, it was so motionless. It opened its topaz eyes, looked at Jury warily, and went back to dozing. Molly Singer's black hair and amber eyes were like the cat's.

They still had not sat down, and she was turning the card he had slipped under the door round and round in her fingers. "You took a chance, didn't you, writing this message? 'What fresh hell can this be?'" Her smile was strained. "Who said it?"

"Dorothy Parker. Whenever she heard the bell to her flat."

"Sit down, won't you?"

The cat glared at Jury as Molly Singer picked it up and put it on one of the cold sling chairs.

She offered him a drink and, when he accepted, reached down into the cabinet by the couch and brought out another glass and a whiskey bottle that was three-fourths empty. She gave him his and replenished her own glass.

Jury felt strange in this room that had housed so many guests, like a room full of ghosts. A log crumbled and the fire spurted up, one of the ghosts stirring the ashes.

"It's the cape, I guess."

Jury had been avoiding this sudden plunge into the death of Angela Thorne. He nodded. "Constable Green recognized it."

"Which puts me in the thick of it, doesn't it?"

"You must have known the cape would be traced to you. Why'd you do it?"

"You mean, kill her?" Her equanimity was more disturbing than a screaming denial would have been.

"I didn't say you killed Angela Thorne. It would be stupid to do that and leave that sort of evidence behind. What happened?"

"I was walking along the Cobb somewhere around ten or ten-thirty. I heard a dog barking. It sounded rather terrible, you know, panic-stricken. I followed the sound to the rocks and found her. I returned the dog; I couldn't return Angela," she said with some bitterness.

"Did you know her?"

Molly shook her head. "I think I saw her once or twice. I don't actually know anyone."

"How do you live?"

Her smile was no more happy than her laughter. "I bolt the door, Superintendent."

"You've lived here nearly a year. Why? Do you like the sea, then?"

"No. In a storm the waves crash over the walls; sometimes even drenching the cottages. Throwing up seaweed, rocks, whatever. It's all so elemental."

"So you found the body, covered her with your cape, took the dog to the Thorne cottage. Is that all?"

"Yes."

"But you rang up the police anonymously. Why?"

"I didn't want to get involved, I suppose."

"Then why did you leave your cape? You must have been freezing."

"I have another one," she said simply, as if that explained everything.

"Where did you live before?"

"London, different places. No fixed address. No job. I've got some money still. I used to be a photographer. My doctor advised me to find some nice little seaside town. I was taking pictures of Lyme."

Jury looked at two fine photos above the mantel: the Lyme coast, the Marine Parade, with its lonely strollers.

She left the couch and walked over to those pictures. "Don't bother looking; I'm not much good anymore. The sea, the sea — it's so elemental." Her glass was empty, and she poured herself another double. "I drink too much, you've noticed." She shrugged and went back to the mantel. The light from the fire suffused her face, sparked the strange dark gold eyes and gave her an almost daemonic look. He thought of the women of myths whom the ill-fated stranger — knight or country yokel — was constantly being warned to steer clear of.

"Have you been reading the papers?" Jury asked. She shook her head. "Where were you earlier today?"

"Here. I'm always here. Why?"

"There was a boy killed in Wynchcoombe. And two days ago, one killed in Dorchester. You didn't know about the Dorchester business?"

Her eyes had a drowned look. "My God, no. What are you saying — that there's a mass-murderer running round the countryside?"

"There could be. Look, there's no way you can avoid talking to police. You don't want to go to the station. Then come along to the White Lion in the morning." He was silent, looking at her, all sorts of sham comfort trying to form itself into words: *it won't be bad; Macalvie is a nice chap; there'll only be the three of us.* All of it lies. It *would* be bad; Macalvie was *not* a nice chap. And "only three of them" might as well be the whole Dorset police and Devon-Cornwall constabulary together, as far as Molly Singer was concerned.

The silence waited on her. "Nine?" was all she said.

"All right."

Jury picked up his coat, once again dislodging the cat from its slumbers — and Molly went with him to the door.

She was still holding the card, folded and refolded, as if it were a message in a bottle that might give some report of land.

NINE

"GEORGE Thorne." In the dining room of the White Lion, Macalvie speared a sausage and shook his head. "One and the same. Witness for the prosecution."

"That doesn't make it look good for Sam Waterhouse, does it?"

"He didn't do it. Pass the butter, Wiggins."

Both Wiggins and Macalvie were having the full house. Jury, who couldn't stick looking at sausages and bacon and eggs, had ordered coffee and toast. "Who'd have a better motive?"

"Someone else," said Macalvie, with perfect assurance.

"But, sir —" Wiggins began and then stopped when Macalvie shot him a look.

"Both of you seem to have forgotten one salient detail. It wasn't Waterhouse that found the kid and tossed a cape over her. Oh, sure. Thorne was ranting on about Waterhouse out for revenge, et cetera. The guy looked like he'd just risen from the grave. Serves the bastard right. Big-deal solicitor." Macalvie was busy with bacon and a reappraisal of the waitress whose Edwardian looks — black hair rolled upward, slim figure in ruffled white blouse and black skirt, and porcelain skin — he had already commented upon. "Yesterday, Angela Thorne was 'acting up' — her mum's words — and trying to plead off school by saying she was sick to her stomach and being a pill nobody wants to swallow. Her teacher said the kid had got into a fight because some other girls were making fun of her. They made up this song: 'Angela Thorne, Angela Thorne, don't you wish you'd never been born? Kids are so cute, aren't they?"

"It was after one when you talked to the Thornes. When did you get a chance to talk to the teacher, for God's sakes?" Jury imagined Macalvie was one of those cops who never slept.

"Afterwards. Let me tell you, the Thornes don't go down a treat. The teacher I knocked up around three —" Macalvie's blue eyes glinted "— you know what that means in American? Anyway Miss Elgin — Julie — didn't especially enjoy having her door busted down by the Devon-Cornwall constabulary, not with her dressed only in a flimsy wrapper —"

"You make it sound like a gang rape, Macalvie. Maybe Wiggins could just read the notes."

Disinclined as he was to stop eating his boiled egg, Wiggins put down his spoon and took out his notebook.

"Put that away, dammit," said Macalvie. "*I* know who said what. So, the kids made up this silly song, mostly, I imagine, because *The Thorn Birds* has been putting everybody to sleep for days now on the telly. You know; it's that mini-mind soap opera series. Julie —"

Macalvie could get on a first-name basis pretty quickly, Jury thought.

"— said Angela got a real going over with that pun on her name. None of the kids much liked Angela Thorne. Why?" Macalvie answered his own question. "Because she was sullen, bad-tempered, plain as pudding, wore thick glasses, and was so good at her lessons it even tired out the teachers. Julie said the headmistress just wished Angela'd take her O levels and get the hell out. Pretty funny." Whatever Macalvie was remembering from the night before obviously delighted him.

"Not very funny for Angela. Wasn't this Julie Elgin a little cut up over Angela's murder?"

"Sure. Scared witless, like everybody else. News travels fast. At midnight parents were calling her to say their kids wouldn't be going to school. But the point is, nobody liked Angela, including her parents."

Jury put down his coffee cup. "Her teacher said that?"

"No. And she didn't have to, did she?" Again he answered his rhetorical question. "Mummy's eyes were red, but more from booze than from tears. George was more worried about his own neck than his kid's death, though of course, he put up a front — but it was all pretense, no pain — and the older sister, the one who got the looks, kept talking about being in shock, as if she'd like to go into it for my sake, but couldn't get the electrodes in place. In other words, it was all an act. I asked them for a picture of Angela. Mum and Dad kind of looked at one another as if they couldn't quite place their youngest, and finally Carla — the sister — had to go off and *look* for a picture. Funny. There were certainly pictures of the bosomy rose Carla all over the mantel. But not even so much as a snapshot of Angela."

"Then she must have been a lonely little girl. Let's get back to your theory of what happened."

"Well, it's the dog, isn't it?" Macalvie watched Jury lighting a cigarette as if it were a daemonic act, meant to trap Macalvie into reaching for the packet.

"The dog? Macalvie, if you say something about the dog in the nighttime, I'll do just what you want — leave." Jury smiled.

Macalvie's hopeful look vanished when Jury didn't actually get up. Then he shrugged: stay or leave, it was all one to Macalvie. "The person who killed the kid must have had some connection with her or Lyme Regis. How the hell did he or she know where to drop the dog?"

"Dogtags, maybe."

Macalvie looked pained. "Oh, for Christ's sake, Jury. A perfect stranger wandering all over Lyme carrying a terrier looking for Cobble Cottage? No way. So it was either someone who befriended the Kid and the Poor Kid's dog," (Jury could just feel the sympathy welling up in Macalvie's breast) "someone not from Lyme, or someone who's been *living* in Lyme and knew the kid's habits."

"But Angela Thorne didn't habitually go against the rules, you led me to believe."

Impatiently, Macalvie stuffed a sourball in his mouth, sucked on it awhile as he hankered after Jury's cigarette, then tossed the candy in the ashtray. "Wonder how Kojak stood it. . . .Look at little Angela's feelings about Mum and Dad and school and so forth. Somebody could have befriended her and then hung around Lyme, waiting for a chance. What do you think?"

"I think no." Jury would have laughed had Macalvie not looked so serious. Disagree with Macalvie's theory?

"Why the hell *not?*"

"Aren't you overlooking the obvious?"

Macalvie gave Wiggins a *can-you-believe-this-guy?* look, got no reassurance from Jury's sergeant, and turned the sparking blue eyes back to Jury. "I never overlooked the *obvious* in my entire life, Jury."

"That's swell. You do think Angela was killed by the same person that murdered the other two, don't you?"

"Probably," said Macalvie, cautiously, like a man being led into a trap.

"Then you'd have to assume that the murderer was friendly with *all* of the victims. That's possible, but not very probable. I don't think the murders are indiscriminate or arbitrary, but at the same time, I don't think the killer took the chance of 'befriending' these children. Simply because it would have been a hell of a chance to take —"

"True. Especially for a man just out of prison."

And since Macalvie's theory left only one candidate for the string of murders, it was perhaps less than fortuitous for her that Molly Singer chose that moment to appear in the doorway of the White Lion's dining room.

II

It wasn't love at first sight when Molly Singer met Divisional Commander Macalvie.

The sparks between them made Jury think of a high-speed train braking. She could sense Macalvie's hostility, even before he opened his mouth.

Jury offered her breakfast, and Macalvie offered her a grim-reaper smile, which was enough to kill anyone's appetite. Jury doubted she had one to begin with. She asked for coffee.

Today she looked different. Her eyes were less molten gold and more honey-colored. That might have been because of the gold cape she wore. Her dark hair was pulled back, but the shorter ends clung to her face as if they were wet with seaspray or rain.

"I just wanted to have a little talk with you about last night," said Macalvie. "Your handling of the situation was kind of odd."

"Yes, I suppose it was. Though at the time I wasn't thinking too clearly —"

"Did you panic, or something?" His tone was almost friendly.

"Panic. Yes, I suppose you could say that."

"That's why you threw your cape over the girl?"

She nodded and looked away.

"Not because you wanted to hide the body." The tone was simply matter-of-fact.

Quickly, she looked at him again. "That's ridiculous. If I'd killed her, I certainly wouldn't leave my cape behind to lead police right to my door."

Macalvie shrugged. "You're not the only one in Lyme or hereabouts who owns a cape."

"You think I'd take a chance like that?"

"I don't know. Do you know the Thornes?"

She shook her head, looking down at the coffee brought by the patrician waitress, but not drinking it.

"How did you know where to take the dog?"

"The name of their place was on the tag."

"Very humanitarian. There's a pub in Dorchester called the Five Alls. Ever been there?"

"No. I don't go to pubs."

"Not a drinker?"

"On the contrary, I drink a lot. But alone."

Wiggins, who seemed to have taken a liking to Molly Singer as another victim of life's vicissitudes, looked sad. Jury was afraid he might take them all for a stroll down Gin Lane.

"As I'd guess," Molly went on, "you already know."

Macalvie's eyes grew round as a cat's. "How would I know that?"

She looked at Jury. "The superintendent might have told you. More likely you've already been at the dustbin men."

Macalvie laughed. "You're pretty smart." He made it sound like an indictment. "Where were you early yesterday morning? Around six, say?"

"In my cottage. Asleep. Why?"

"And where the afternoon of the tenth?"

"In my cottage. Or walking on the Cobb."

"Like last night?"

"Yes."

"Anyone see you?"

"Probably not."

"You don't go out much."

"No."

"You don't see people."

"No."

"Funny way to act."

"I think I'm agoraphobic." What there was of an embarrassed smile was quickly erased when Macalvie slammed his fist on the table.

"I don't care sod-all about some phobia. If you've been to psychiatrists, I'll subpoena their records if I have to. You don't go out, don't see people, and yet —" Macalvie pointed toward the street "— in that short-stay parking lot by the ocean you've got a great little Lamborghini that's clocked up over sixty thousand on a 'C' registration. You do a hell of a lot of traveling, don't you? In that car you could make it to Dorchester and back in a little more than an hour and to Wynchcoombe in two, I'll bet — provided a cop didn't get in your way. What's a little stay-at-home like you doing with a Lamborghini?"

Molly Singer got up slowly. "I think I've answered your questions."

"No, you haven't. Sit down."

"Wouldn't you rather finish your breakfast?" Before anyone could stop her, she tipped her side of the table, sending plates, food, cutlery crashing and rolling, and most of it into Macalvie's lap. Then she walked out.

"God! What a temper." Macalvie seemed perversely pleased, looking at his stained suit and the wreckage all around them: cups, kippers, broken glass.

It even broke the porcelain pose of the waitress in black and white.

III

Lyme Regis was one of many coastal villages whose beauty was reckoned in proximity to the sea. It had been two centuries ago so much the object of Jane Austen's affections that it now had, where the Marine Parade ended in a narrow street, a pretty boutique called Persuasion. Thought Jury, If Stratford-upon-Avon wants to put Shakespeare on sugar cubes . . . why not?

Macalvie came out of the newsagent's at the top of the street, at the triangle where Broad Street and Silver Street ran together down to the sea, taking tearooms, greengrocers, Boots, and banks with them. Wiggins had been left to see to the wreckage at the White Lion.

Just as Macalvie appeared, a Mini went speedboating down the narrow street. He wrote the registration number in his notebook. Macalvie would do dog's duty just so long as it gave him the pleasure of collaring some miscreant.

He slapped the notebook shut and said, "Nothing there. She knew Angela because Angela would stand around reading *Chips and Whizzer* without paying. The old broad in there hated her. She chased her off yesterday evening somewhere around six. She was closing up late."

Macalvie was turning a stile of postcards and removed one that showed the confluence of the streets they were on. He stuffed a stick of gum in his mouth, and said, "You're a minder, you know?"

Jury looked at Macalvie, who was frowning down at the postcard. "Meaning what?"

Macalvie shrugged. "A minder: kind of cop who watches over frails. Defenseless women."

Jury laughed. "You see too many American films, Macalvie."

Unoffended, Macalvie said, "No, I'm serious."

Indeed he did look it, staring from the picture-view of the street to the real thing. One would have thought he might be an artist, studying light and angles. "I'd like to know what she's doing in Lyme," he said, almost inconsequentially.

"Molly Singer?"

He shook his head. "Her name's not Molly Singer. It's Mary Mulvanney."

Macalvie slotted the card back in the rack and started up the street.

IV

The St. Valentine's Day Massacre

TEN

THE Lady Jessica Mary Allan-Ashcroft looked from blank square to blank square on the calendar hanging in the kitchen and with her black crayon, stood on tiptoe so she could reach FRIDAY: 14 FEBRUARY. She drew a giant X across that square, knowing she was cheating, since it was only teatime and the awful day was not yet over. Another day as blank as the square. There were now five X's in a row. The picture above them showed some Dartmoor ponies doing what they always did — chewing grass. She looked at the picture for March. It showed the giant rock-formation of Vixen Tor and a few hardy pilgrims on their way up the rocks. Another stupid pile of rocks they walked for miles to see.

Just last August she had been driving out with Uncle Robert and had seen a lot of people with boots and back packs at one of those tourist centers, all kitted out to walk to one of those tors in the middle of Dartmoor. Jessie and her uncle were driving with the top down in his Zimmer, and she thought those people out there must be crazy, walking when they could be driving. She told him this and he burst out laughing.

* * *

"Eat your tea, my love," said Mrs. Mulchop. Her husband, Mulchop, served as groundskeeper and sometimes as butler and looked no more like one than he did the other. He sat now at the kitchen table eating a mess of something.

Mrs. Mulchop moved a pot in the huge inglenook fireplace, in the huge kitchen, in the huge house, in the huge grounds. . . .

Jessie's mind drifted like a veil of rain over all of this hugeness that was the Ashcroft house and grounds. "It's too big," she said, looking at the egg on toast on her plate. Its sickening yellow eye stared back at her.

"Your egg, lovey?"

"No. The house. I'm all alone." Jessie rested her chin in her hands.

Mrs. Mulchop raised her eyes heavenward and shook her head. She did not realize that beneath this surface melodrama, a true drama of heartsickness was playing itself out. "You're ten years old, not a baby. Wouldn't your uncle be annoyed to see you so sorry for yourself?"

Jessie was shocked to think that anyone would believe Uncle Robert would ever be "annoyed" by Jessie. "No! He'd understand." Now Jessie felt the threat of real tears. Real tears she could not contend with.

"Your uncle's only been gone a few days, lass. No need to get fidgety about it —"

"*Four* days! Four and a *half!* See —" Jessie scraped her chair back and marched to the calendar. "He didn't leave me a note. He didn't give me a Valentine, either." She went back to her chair as if she'd just proven all theories of a clockwork universe defunct in the face of this outrage against reason. But what she felt was more worry than outrage.

"He's probably only gone up to London to see to another governess for you." Mrs. Mulchop glanced at her husband, but his face was too near his bowl to return the look.

Jessie heard the slight sharpness in that *another*. She ran through governesses like a shark through a salmon-fall.

"And you're not all alone. There's me and Mulchop and Miss Gray and Drucilla."

The Dreadful Drucilla, Miss Plunkett, the present tutor-governess. Not a proper one, though. More of a minder Uncle Rob had settled for when he had discharged the Careless Carla, who was absolutely brilliant at maths, but a little absentminded about keys and spectacles. Out walking across the moor, she had lost Jessie one day, though there had been, in the confrontation with Robert Ashcroft, some doubt as to who had lost whom.

Battalions of governesses. How they sat so neatly and nicely when he was interviewing them. Uncle Rob questioned them closely about their former posts, their credentials, their ability to respond to emergencies; but now and then he would throw one in from left field, such as *And do you like rabbits?*

Jessie liked to see the corners of his mouth twitch and the bewildered look on the face of the prospective employee. *Well, yes. That is, I expect I've nothing against them. . . .* He had explained later to Jess that it was a matter of honesty, and Miss Whatever-her-name wasn't being honest. She was from Portland (where the Ashcroft stone had come from). *In Portland, one is never allowed to mention rabbits. They all hate them,* Uncle Rob had told her.

Thus that one had lost out on a very well paying post, as did most of the prospective women who applied. They sat there saying, *Oh, yes, Mr. Ashcroft,* when they meant No; or *Oh, no, Mr. Ashcroft,* when they meant Yes. And a lot of them would try to snuggle up to Jessica until they realized she wasn't much good for a snuggle, and call her stupid things like "Poppit," and pet her dog Henry, to show how much they liked animals.

Robert Ashcroft could not go on forever relentlessly pursuing the perfect governess, so in the end, he left it up to Jessie, as she was the one who would have to put up with the woman. Uncle Rob often asked her why it was she avoided the nicer ones and chose the worst. There was the Hopeless Helen (who kept the key to the drinks cabinet in more or less constant motion); the Mad Margaret, who had trembled during the interview with a severe case of stage fright, but ended up roaring like a lion, acting being her field of expertise; the Prudent Prucilla, who left rather quickly one night, along with the Crown Derby. Of all of them, the Dubious Desiree had lasted the longest because she had done nothing absolutely wrong, short of hating her pupil, a fact that she kept very well hidden from everyone but Jess herself. Jess put up with the cold-blooded treatment because she knew Desiree was going to do herself in anyway, eventually. In the meantime, she did make Jess a little nervous because of her looks: she was dark and sleek and always winding herself on the couch like a cobra when he was around. But Uncle Rob was not easily fooled; the Dubious Desiree lasted a month.

It seemed a great puzzle to Uncle Rob — his niece's choices. Why Miss Simpson instead of Miss James? *Miss Simpson seemed a bit stiff to me. But Sally James was, well, rather smashing,* he said, before he had returned to the reading of his morning paper, the jamming of his morning toast.

Jessie was not about to have any Smashing Sallys around.

Thus Jessie had never complained about any of them because she knew, every time one of them got sacked, there might be another just waiting in the wings. The Amiable Amy.

Jessie was an omnivorous reader — largely owing to Mad Margaret, who stuffed books and plays into her like sausage. Mad Margaret thought herself the heroine of all of them. Many was the rainy morning that found Jess curled up on the window seat in the library with Henry as a backrest, poring over *Jane Eyre* and *Rebecca*. Jessie knew just how sly some women could be: soft and kind and quiet-spoken and so sly (and amiable) they might even catch Jessie in their nets.

Her uncle had once been married — years and years ago — to a dazzling but false woman who had broken his heart, left him shattered with grief — or, at least, that was the way she put it to him at the breakfast table. "I know it must have left you shattered. You can never look at another woman, can you?"

He did not seem, as he slit open the morning post, terribly shattered. This was, unfortunately, confirmed when he said, "No — I mean to the 'shattered' part of your tale. As to the rest, I think I could bear to look at another woman again, yes. God knows I've looked at enough of them trying to find some-one for you."

She had placed a consoling hand on his arm. "But she was beautiful, wasn't she?"

"Indeed she was. But she hated motorcars." He smiled.

"But she loved you madly."

"Not really." He went back to his paper.

All of those governesses over the four years they'd been at Ashcroft. Look what they would get: wealth, position, the glories of Ashcroft itself — to say nothing of one of the most eligible bachelors in the British Isles. And nine motor cars.

The only thing that stood between them and Heaven was Lady Jessica Allan-Ashcroft.

II

The funeral had been held in a parish, the body committed to the ground of a leaf-strewn cemetery in Chalfont St. Giles, where her father had been born and where Jessica's mother had died years ago. Her father had been the Earl of Curlew and Viscount Linley, James Whyte Ashcroft; her mother, plain Barbara Allan, but plain in name only. And between them they had passed on their names to Jessica.

When her father died, Jessie was six years old, and mere days before this she had been chasing her dog, Henry, all over the grounds of the old home in Chalfont.

They had dressed her in mourning. An aunt with eager fingers had affixed the boater with its black ribbon to her head, placed the gloves in her hand. Jessie did not know the aunt, nor any of the cousins — a great ring of them around the grave — nor anyone except for a few of her father's old friends.

She was dead silent, but Jessie wanted to scream when the vicar went on about Heaven and Rewards. She did not think her father would be tempted by Rewards. He would rather be back here with Jessie.

All around her stood those odd friends and relations, as stark and unmoving as pollarded trees. All in black and dreadful, some with heavy veils, or, hats in hands, expressions frozen, like skaters on a dark lake. One hand fell on her shoulder. She shook it off. The fingers felt like claws. When she looked all round the grave-site again, she saw red-rimmed eyes, not sorrow-laden, but the eyes of wolves.

Jessica Allan-Ashcroft was worth four million pounds to them. And that didn't even include the family seat of Ashcroft.

Just as the service ended, she noticed a stranger in a light-colored Burberry. The mourners were going through the awful ritual of throwing a handful of earth on her father's grave. The stranger walked through the dark stalks of mourners, knelt down and brushed the blown strands of hair from her face. *"Cry,"* was all he said, but in such a tone that her mind split and the tears gushed out. In his own face, she saw something of her father's and even her own and she threw her arms around him and buried her face in his raincoat.

Solicitors were wandering everywhere, in and out of the house in Eaton Square, like dream figures. There were more relations to come, too, others whom Jessie didn't know, coming with long faces, bringing her things she didn't want and calling her "love" and "dear" and none of them meaning it, she knew.

The day after the funeral — to her it had seemed like months — she stood before the long window in the house in Eaton Square, wondering if the man in the raincoat would ever come back. The trees dripped rain and Henry looked up at her with red-rimmed eyes, a true mourner.

Everyone seemed to be keeping a vigil. The relations had gathered in the library with her father's solicitor, all of them coughing gently behind their hands.

When finally he did come, running across the road in the rain, Jessie ran to the door and listened. She heard voices in the hall, an exchange between the butler and the stranger, and then all was quiet again.

Until the will was read.

The solicitor, a plump man whose jowls reminded her of Henry, took her hands in his plump, perspiring ones and explained "the situation."

It was boring to Jessie, all of this talk about money and property. The important thing was who her guardian was to be. As if on cue, a large woman and her smaller husband came through the door. The woman was the same one who had laid her hand in such a proprietary way on Jessie's shoulder. Her fingers flashed with rings and the poor fox-fur around her neck flashed its glass eyes. Jessie could tell, with one look, she wasn't an animal-lover. "What about Henry?" she asked.

Mr. Mack, the solicitor, found that very funny. "Now you do understand, Jessie. All of your mother's property was left to you and your father. Now all of it goes to you. You must have someone to look after you."

The large, ring-studded cousin snorted, saying it should be her and Al to do the looking-after, and Mr. Mack asked her to leave. Her husband told her there was no use crying over spilt milk, and to come along.

Through the door then came the man from the cemetery.

Mr. Mack told her that this was her Uncle Robert, her father's brother, Robert Ashcroft. Her father had appointed him trustee of the estate and Jessica's guardian.

"Henry's, too," said Robert Ashcroft, winking.

Thus amongst the raised voices that seemed to be calling for Robert Ashcroft's blood, or at least his bona fides, after his ten-year absence in Australia, Jessie felt as if, on the verge of drowning, she had broken the water's surface, dazzled by sunlight. His hair was dark gold and his eyes were light brown. As the thunder of the others' voices receded, Jessie felt the sun falling in shafts across the room and that all those vaults were really full of gold.

ELEVEN

T HE "letters" — they were what prevented the relations, some inarticulate, some artful — from breaking the will. Her father had been clever enough to leave tiny bequests to those relations whom he disliked (which meant most of them), acknowledging that they were "family," but sorry they were his. It was a little like leaving a small tip for poor service.

It was a very large family, but not a close one. "When I left for Australia over ten years ago, I was thirty" her uncle had told her. "In all of those thirty years before, I can't remember seeing any of these relations who've descended like vultures."

The vultures had flown after months of talking about "undue influence" and "unsound mind," and Jessie and Uncle Robert were sitting in the drawing room in Eaton Square, its furnishings flooded with April sunlight. "Undue influence." He laughed. "It would have been hard to have influenced your father in any case. So how was I supposed to have done it all the way from Australia? Ten years of letters." Robert had stopped and looked at his niece intently. "Jimmy — your father — in any event, how was I supposed to have done it all the way from Australia? Ten years of letters . . ." He had stopped and then said, "It doesn't make you sad, I hope, talking about your father?"

"No. I want to hear about him. And Mother, too." Henry was lying between them, being used as an armrest. "Go on."

"There must have been, over the course of ten years, hundreds of letters. Jimmy was having a hard time of it after your mother died." He paused, thinking back. "And before that, even. He was depressed . . . I don't know if it was because he felt some sort of prescience of Barbara's death, or what. I felt guilty leaving. But I had to."

"Why?"

He was quiet. "I just had to. Anyway, those letters showed we'd kept in touch. You know, when I was at a perfectly awful public school, when I was ten and Jimmy was twenty and my life was hell, he wrote to me three or four times a week. He knew how miserable I was. That's really something for a chap of twenty to do for a boy of ten."

Jessie had managed to circumvent the baggage of Henry to lean across and put her head on her uncle's shoulder. "You were mates. I bet when you were six he got into fights because the boys teased you and threw things at your dog and made fun of you and called you names. Didn't he?" Her tone was hopeful.

"Absolutely."

"Tell me about Mother," she commanded.

"She was beautiful. Dark hair and eyes. You look just like her."

So that her uncle wouldn't see her blush, she busied herself in trying to tie Henry's ears together. A difficult job, since they were hard to find.

"Talk about getting teased over your name! 'Barbara Allan' is an old folk song," said Robert.

"What about?" Henry awoke and shook at his ears.

Robert didn't answer at first, and Jess poked him. She refused to let any important question — meaning any of hers — go unanswered.

"About Sweet William's dying because he loved her."

It was the way he said it. Jessie didn't like his silence. "I've got a picture!" She bounced up, unsettling the cushions and comfort, much to Henry's displeasure. "I keep it locked up."

"Locked up? But why?"

Because she had always had a secret fear that if too many eyes saw her mother's picture, her mother would grow less clear, less distinct, the outlines blurring into the background until the beautiful face of Barbara Allan disappeared altogether. The worst was that Jessie was one of them. If she looked too long, the face in the picture would go away, as her mother had done. But she couldn't tell *him* such a stupid, silly thing. Jess went over to the ebony desk and took a key from a vase and turned it in the bottom drawer. It was only a snapshot. The woman there was kneeling in long grass, gathering wildflowers. Peering through the long grass was a funny-looking puppy.

"That's Henry," she said with feigned disgust. "I wish he hadn't followed her around like that. He made her trip once — I saw it — and she fell down. It could've *killed* her. He was a bad dog." She looked quickly at Henry to see if he might contradict her. "But Henry's okay, now." It was with a growing horror that she saw the weight she'd been carrying for years. She was afraid she'd done something to her mother. Killed her by being born, maybe.

And Robert knew. He put his hands on her shoulders and said, harshly, "Listen to me! You didn't do anything to hurt your mother, Jess. She looked healthy and was much younger than your father. But she was still a sick woman."

Jessie looked down at her mother's picture, the awful weight lifted from her shoulders. She rubbed the glass carefully, delicately, with the hem of her skirt. Then she set the picture atop the desk. Her mother wouldn't disappear just because Jessie looked at her too long.

But she was still embarrassed that her uncle had figured all of this out about her when she'd only just found it out herself. "I think it's time for Henry's walk," she said, smoothly. *Henry's walk* would have been only an annual event, had exercising him been left to Jess.

"Mind if I come?"

"Oh, I guess not. But Henry will only listen to *me*. So it's no use you trying to make him catch sticks, or anything. He won't unless I command him."

It was no use *anyone's* trying to make Henry catch sticks, as Jess perfectly well knew.

II

Thus here she was, four years later, four years of picnics and open motor cars; and trains to London and Brighton; and Careless Clara and all the rest of the benighted ladies. Here she was musing over the past, while Mrs. Mulchop kept to the present, wrist-deep in dough.

Jessie leaned a cold cheek against her fist and punched the spoon down into the equally cold porridge with which Mrs. Mulchop had replaced the egg. And Jess let it sit there like the egg. It had hardened to such a thickness, the spoon stuck straight up. "He never goes off without leaving me a note or something." It was the dozenth time she'd imparted the same information in different ways.

"Well, lovey, he just forgot this time —"

Forgot? Was Mrs. Mulchop crazy?

"— and he has to have his bit of fun, now doesn't he? Do you begrudge the man that, my lady? Think of him, not yourself: a man in his forties always in company of a ten-year-old —" The look in My Lady's eye changed her tune quickly. "— not that you're not fun. But your uncle should have a nice wife to look after —"

"He doesn't *want* one. He already *had* one." Jess had left the kitchen table and was taking down an overall from a peg by the back door. "It left him a broken man." She stuffed her legs into the overall.

" 'Broken man'? *Your* uncle? He's about as broke as Mulchop here."

Mulchop looked up from his huge bowl. He was bull-necked and stout-armed and had a spatulate face, flat as the spades he used on the flowers and shrubs. He seldom spoke and appeared to resent it if others engaged in conversation. Words were wasted on Mulchop.

"Where's the spanner?" Jessica leveled her eyes at his thick brows.

The spoon, which had but an inch to travel from bowl to mouth, stopped. "You not be foolin' with them cars, Miss!" Mulchop also took care of the cars; he and Jessie spent what little time they spent together haggling over Uncle Robert's cars.

While Mrs. Mulchop went prattling on about Mr. Robert's sad marital status, Jessie took the spanner from Mulchop's tool box and stuck her tongue out at both of their backs.

". . . a nice wife, that's what he needs."

Not if the Lady Jessica Mary Allan-Ashcroft had anything to do with it.

She lay with the spanner and some old rags on a mechanic's creeper underneath the Zimmer Golden Spirit. It was a good car for thinking under; some of the others, like the Lotus and the Ferrari were a little too close to the ground for her to get comfortable unless she jacked them up, and Mulchop would always come out and raise a fuss. The Zimmer was one of her favorites, an astonishingly long white convertible, for which Uncle Robert had paid over thirty thousand pounds. Or Jess had paid. It took a platoon of solicitors to keep account of her money. Not that it made any difference to her if Uncle Robert used up all of it on his cars.

Jessie saw a bolt that looked loose and she tried to tighten it. That's what happened when someone went away.... Everything just fell apart. Her eyes widened. Forgetting where she was she sat up and bumped her forehead on the exhaust pipe. The cars.

"Well, *I* don't know, do I?" the Dreadful Dru was saying, as Jess stood there in the drawing room in her oil-stained overall. "You been muckin' about with those cars?"

"They're all *there!*" Jessie shouted. In a sort of ritual chant, she ticked off each one of the nine on her fingers.

Drucilla Plunkett tossed aside the fashion magazine she'd been reading and stuffed another chocolate in her mouth. Drucilla knew her days were numbered, so she wasn't being at all careful about what she did with them. The box of chocolates — a huge heart — Drucilla had said she'd got from an "admirer" down the pub. Most of her spare time was spent with one or another mystery man "down the pub," as she put it. "What do I know about those old cars?" Her bowlike mouth bit into a chocolate truffle.

"If he went to London, how did he go?"

"Say it once again and I'll *scream!*"

Jessie said she could scream the house down. All she wanted to know was where Uncle Rob was. "He's missing." Jessie turned and leaned her forehead against the cold glass, saw the ghost of her face in the slanting rain.

The Dreadful Dru screamed. Not long and loud, but a shriek nonetheless. Having exhausted her eyes with the latest fashions, Drucilla was now exhausting her mind with a newspaper. "God!" She sat up straight. "Look here, there's a prisoner let out of Princetown several days ago. The Ax-murderer — that's what they call him."

Drucilla's little scream might have come from the ghost out in the rain, trying to get in.

* * *

Nobody cared, that was clear.

Victoria Gray was a cousin educated well beyond the means of the jobs that might have come her way. Thus Jess's father had employed her in the ambiguous role of "house-keeper," and Victoria did perform what duties she could find. With Mrs. Mulchop, Mulchop, and Billy (the stable-lad), the household was top-heavy with servants. Victoria's servitude was minimal, the line between housekeeper and long-standing guest somewhat blurred.

"Wonder how old she is?" Uncle Robert had said one morning before they had moved from Eaton Square to Ash-croft. He was slitting open the morning post, letter after letter from banks and solicitors. "I believe we've inherited Victoria along with the heirlooms. Still, she's all right." He stopped in the act of opening a letter and said, reflectively, "Actually, she's quite attractive."

Because Victoria Gray had been around ever since Jessie could remember, she hadn't expected trouble from that quarter. "Fifty," she said, beheading her boiled egg smartly with the clipper.

Robert frowned. "Fifty? Surely not. She doesn't look forty to me. Did she tell you, then?"

Jessie had looked at him with cool eyes. "Would *you* tell if you were that old?" With her uncle looking at her that way, now she would have to come up with an explanation as to how she knew Victoria's age. Inspired by the letters lying on the table, she said, "It was a birthday card. She left it on a table. There was a great, big fifty —" Here Jess drew a 5 and 0 in the air, huge numbers, in case her uncle thought fifty wasn't all that much. Satisfied, she dipped a toast finger in her egg.

Uncle Robert was looking at her with his head slightly cocked. And then came that bemused smile that bothered her. "If that's so, she must take wonderful care of herself."

Jessie concentrated on dabbing tiny bits of plum preserve on her toast. "She does. Victoria has lots of those little pots of colors and jars of cream and stuff. Before she goes to bed she wears the cream and a hair net."

Instead of being put off by this odious picture, he was fascinated and completely forgot about his mail. "Well, she certainly has beautiful skin. It must all pay off."

"That's from the mud."

"Mud?"

"Sometimes ladies put it on their faces when they're old to make their skin tight." Here, Jess pressed her fingers to the sides of her own flawless face, pulling the skin back.

Uncle Rob shook his head. "Poor Victoria. Paint, cream, mud."

Quickly, the *Times* came up in front of his face, but Jessie thought she might have seen just the beginning of a smile, snatched away.

She studied the beads of jam on her toast and wondered if she should have left out the mud.

That evening of the fourteenth, Victoria Gray broke into Jess's reflections on the weather, the fog, the condition of the roads. Night had descended on the moor like a black-gloved hand. But he hadn't take a car — that was the trouble.

"You're being childish, Jess. Better you go to bed and stop all this morbid worrying."

"I *am* a child, aren't I?" A fact she denied most of the time, using it only when it suited her. She watched Victoria collect the balled-up wrappers that the Dreadful Dru had aimed at Henry, now napping on a chair by the fire. He was always napping. She supposed she loved Henry, but he was getting boring.

Victoria was going on about the Dreadful Dru: ". . . glad to see *that* one leave. The only thing she's good at is penmanship. Probably a forger in her youth."

None of them seemed to understand the monumental importance of what had happened. "Did you see him leave?"

Victoria sighed. "*No,* for the tenth time. No. He obviously left early in the morning — he's done it before — when we were all asleep. You know your uncle is impulsive."

But that didn't explain the absence of a Valentine, the lack of a note.

"Jessie, dear." Victoria stood directly behind her now, doubling the reflection in the window. "Go to bed and stop worrying. Can't you allow your uncle to forget just *once* — ?"

"*No!* Come on, Henry!" Jessie ordered the dog before she ran from the room. Henry, looking tired and sad, had to obey this injunction, as it was usually the only one he ever got from his mistress.

But she didn't go to bed directly. First, she took down her yellow slicker from the peg beside the overall and jammed her arms in it before she opened the heavy door leading out to what used to be all horse-boxes.

The stable now provided room for garaging nine cars. There were two horses boxed on the other side. Victoria loved to ride; Jessica hated it. She'd told her uncle there were so many ponies on the moor, just looking at a pony made her want to throw up. And she certainly wasn't going to some stupid riding school, only to go round and round in a ring.

"I want a car," she had said, as his collection grew.

"A *car?* Jess, you're seven years old."

She sighed. How many times had she heard that? "In a month I'll be eight. I want a Mini Cooper. You know. The one Austin Rover made." She was rather proud of having come upon this minuscule bit of information.

"Police don't look kindly on eight-year-olds driving."

* * *

The Mini Cooper was there. Henry slogged behind her, stopping when she stopped. He yawned, unused to this nocturnal inspection of cars in the dark and the rain. Rain blew the hood of her slicker as Jessica walked round the old stables, beaming her torch on each one, touching the bonnet — almost *patting* the car, as if each were indeed a favorite horse.

TWELVE

JESSIE lay in bed in the pre-dawn hours, with Henry like a heavy duvet at her feet. She stared up at the tracery of light that the blowing branches etched on the ceiling. Then she turned on her side. Instead of counting sheep (which was horribly dull), she started counting off the rooms at Ashcroft. Her thoughts lingered on the long, dark hall beyond her bedroom door, and on Uncle Rob's room, two doors down, full of leather and chairs and books and a high mahogany chest where he kept the pictures of her father and mother.

But she couldn't think of that room and sleep. Her mind traveled on to Dreadful Dru's — the room on the other side of hers. Dru was living the life of Laura Ashley (which didn't fit her a bit) — tiny flowers on wallpaper, tiny sprigs on curtains that made Jessie think of thorn-thickets. Whenever she went into the Dreadful Dru's room, she felt trapped by stinging nettles. Next to Dru was Victoria Gray, whose room matched her perfectly. It was rather mysterious, with its silky velvet drapes that lay in heavy folds upon the floor.

None of this was helping her sleep. She counted the rooms in the servants' wing where Mr. and Mrs. Mulchop and Billy had their rooms. The other six rooms in that wing were empty.

Like a potential buyer viewing a property, her mind was led down the dark hall outside her room and down the sweeping Adam staircase to what was now a well of darkness: the big entry room that on sunny days was bright, its floor of Spanish tiles, its circular table in the center pungent with the smells of roses or jasmine.

She opened her eyes and saw that the black panes had lightened to purple. The casement windows rattled in rain. Jessie turned on her other side and took her mind through the tiled hall, into the morning room where, at the dreary age of twenty or so, she would most likely have to talk to people like the local vicar or Major Smythe. . . .

"I don't want to grow up," she had told Uncle Robert a year ago. "To get old like sixteen and have to go to some boring boarding school like All Hallows."

It was a misty September morning. They had taken the Zimmer and a basket of lunch to Haytor.

Jess had held her breath, waiting for him to say something like *But you must grow up,* or *You'll love school.* Only, he couldn't say that, could he? Not after his own awful schooldays.

What he did say was, "I don't see why you have to do anything before you feel like it."

She looked up at the sky that had changed from a sluggish gray to clear pearl. "But I *have* to."

"Go away? When you're ready. Otherwise, it just makes misery."

Now she felt adult and indignant at his lack of knowledge of the Real World. "Don't you know people are *always* having to do things they don't like to? Lucy Manners — she had to go to All Hallows whether she liked it or not."

"She's got spots, hasn't she?"

Jessica was trying to be serious. "What's that got to do with it?"

Uncle Rob was lying on the rock, an arm thrown over his face. "Don't they all have spots, the boarding school ones? Either spots or teeth that stick out? I don't think you should go because you're much too pretty. I'd hate to see you with spots and stuck-out teeth."

And she began to think of school in more kindly terms. "Lucy Manners would have spots *anywhere*," she said reasonably.

II

Jessie lay on her back and watched the shadows of the branches comb the ceiling in the gathering light. She was still debating what to do. She got out of bed.

Although Henry had no desire to rout himself from the foot of the warm bed and follow, follow he did. *Come on, Henry,* were the three worst words in the language.

She could not reach the telephone in the kitchen because it was high up on the wall. Jess pulled over the cricket stool that Mulchop liked to sit on and smell the soup cooking.

The operator took forever to answer. Jess hung up twice, each time being careful to dial 100. Finally, she got one of them, frosty, far-off in her wired-up ice castle. Jess cleared her throat. "My name's Jessica Ashcroft and I live at Ashcroft. That's fifteen miles outside Exeter. My uncle's missing. I want the police."

The operator talked to her in that sort of slow, loud way that people used with deaf people and dumb children. When Jessie explained that her uncle had been missing five days, the operator asked her why she thought he was "missing."

"Because he isn't *here!*" Jessie hung up. It was hopeless. How could she ever make the operator understand that he'd never go anywhere without leaving a note — and, especially, a Valentine. Today — well, just yesterday, was St. Valentine's Day. Uncle Rob always remembered every holiday. And how could she make the operator understand about the cars? Jessie leaned against the black telephone and came close to crying. She gulped to stop the tears. Henry shook himself out of his lethargy and pawed at her leg and whined in sympathy. But his eyes closed like shutters and he dozed off again.

While she was sitting on the cricket stool, an image came back to Jessie. It was the Dreadful Dru on the couch, stuffing herself with chocs and trying to read the paper.

Jessie took down the receiver and dialed Emergency — 999. A crisp, no-nonsense voice asked her what she wanted. Ambulance? Hospital? Police?

Jessie lowered her voice a notch, rounded her vowels, and enunciated clearly, in just the way Mad Margaret had taught her. "I am Lady Jessica Allan-Ashcroft." Dramatic pause. "I want Scotland Yard." The telephone nearly slipped from her hand because her palm was so sweaty. Her heart pounded. "That ax-murderer that was released from Dartmoor prison has been to this house and he's killed —" she looked down — "the Honorable Henry Allan-Ashcroft."

Nose on paws, Henry raised beleaguered eyes, unaware that his blood — according to Lady Jessica — was everywhere. Almost total dismemberment. Then he returned to his light doze, equally unaware that he had just been knighted.

All of the operator's questions she had answered cooly, almost indignantly, as if surprised that Lady Jessica Allan-Ashcroft should be questioned by such a menial. Directions were given. Times were given. Names were given. And she hung up, after being told to stay calm.

Calm? With blood running all over the kitchen floor? Was the woman *mad*?

She had begun to believe in her own fantasy until she looked at Henry, lying healthily by the hearth, and wondered how she was going to explain to police how he was so unbloody. And unbowed.

"Come on, Henry. We've got to think."

Henry showed as little inclination for thinking as for following. In the pantry, Jessie found a can of Chum, struggled with the can opener, and put some in a bowl. This she placed on the pantry floor and had no trouble getting Henry in there for his unexpected tea at dawn. She shut the door.

As she walked through the dining room into the drawing room, where morning light lay in splinters on oriental carpets and velvet couches, it occurred to Jessie that the Devonshire police didn't know Henry. And Henry certainly wouldn't talk.

But she, Jessie, would have to. How would she explain the lack of blood? Blood was not easy to come by, and she had no intention of sacrificing any of hers. She sat on the same sofa as had the Dreadful Dru, trying to be calm, trying to think. Jessie looked out the window and saw the cold, scabrous dawn slither up the grass like a snake and considered tomato sauce.

But where was the slaughtered body? Cold in only her nightdress, she still sat there, constructing and reconstructing her story. In the attic was a dressmaker's dummy. If she put it in a dark corner of the kitchen and tossed the tomato sauce all over, she could say she saw it and just went crazy. . . .

Yet, wouldn't that open up more questions? *Who* had put the dummy there and spilt the sauce all round?

At the same time she heard barking from the pantry, she heard the double-note of sirens coming up the gravel drive. The revolving lights, the noise, caused a lot of thumping from the rooms upstairs.

Footsteps coming down the stairs, footsteps coming up the

gravel. She felt sorry for Henry, shut up in the pantry, and sorrier for herself. She was going to have a lot to answer for.

III

The Dreadful Dru came in holding a candlestick, like a left-over from the Mad Margaret's repertoire of characters. But the Dreadful Dru looked more like a blow-fly than she did Lady Macbeth, heavy with sleep in her black peignoir.

Mrs. Mulchop was dressed in her mobcap and brown felt slippers. Victoria Gray in a velvet dressing gown.

Police were everywhere, some in uniform and some in plain clothes; there were also men in white coats, and a doctor with his black bag.

Jessica was surrounded.

There was a torrent of questions and a few shocked answers from Mrs. Mulchop and Victoria Gray. No, they knew nothing. The questions were orchestrated by the insistent barking of Henry. Mrs. Mulchop went to the pantry to investigate.

Jessica scratched at her ear and looked up through squinty eyes as if she couldn't imagine what had brought all this crowd together. The salvo of questions seemed to confuse her awfully, and the man in charge — an Inspector Browne — waited while she gazed all over the ivory and damask splendor of the Ashcroft drawing room. Finally, she asked, "Where am I?"

Drucilla Plunkett was wringing her hands as if to keep them away from Jessica's throat. "Where *are* you? Whatever are you going on about, you silly thing?"

Jessie rubbed her eyes and turned her troubled face to Inspector Browne. "I must've been walking in my sleep again."

Drucilla was yelling now: "You *never* walk in your sleep!"

Jessie considered for a moment. "Yes, I do. You just weren't around."

The logic of this escaped Drucilla, who, having put down the candlestick, raised it now as if she meant to bring it down on her little charge's head. Inspector Browne came between them. The house and grounds were swarming with police.

Nothing, was the report passed back along the line of the inspector's entourage. *Nil*. No body, no blood, no sign of forced entry or anything else. They all looked to Jessie.

"It was a nightmare," said Jessie. "I was having this awful dream about my Uncle Robert. He's been missing —" (and here she looked out of the window to calculate another dawn into the whole of it) "— six days."

Once again Drucilla raised the candlestick. Victoria Gray turned away, looking pained. And the playlet was interrupted by the return of Mrs. Mulchop, marching in with Henry. "And why was Henry closed up in my pantry, I'd like to know, Miss?"

One of Browne's men flipped through a small notebook. "Report was that a Henry Ashcroft had been the victim. The Honorable Henry Allan-Ashcroft."

Before Dru or Victoria or Mrs. Mulchop could react fully to this announcement, Jessie had jumped up from the couch. "*Henry!* You're all *right!*" She flung her arms about the massed wrinkles that were Henry.

They all looked down in wonder. A child and her dog.

THIRTEEN

BRIAN Macalvie seemed at first to be merely irritated by the telephone's ringing at four A.M. in the Lyme Regis station. He cradled the receiver like a bawling baby against his ear. Macalvie might, indeed, have been a new father, thought Jury; he didn't seem to need sleep. They had been all day in Dorchester and Exeter.

As he listened to the voice on the other end, Macalvie stopped sucking the Fisherman's Friend. Wiggins had left the packet before going back to the White Lion for some sleep. In slow motion, Macalvie's feet left the desk that had been supporting them; the chair creaked with his weight as he sat up. He nodded and said, "Yeah, I've got it." He hung up.

Then he put his head in his hands.

"What the hell is it?" asked Jury, surprised by Macalvie's look of remorse.

"Dartmoor. Bloody Dartmoor. It sounds like it's happening all over again."

II

"Dartmoor." Wiggins said it with a shudder as they drove off the A 35 toward Ashburton.

"You'll love it, Wiggins," said Macalvie, "it's got a prison and ponies and it rains sideways."

He was right about the rain. Wiggins was huddled down in his coat in the back seat. "You should slow down a bit, sir. This road's posted as not being appropriate for caravans."

"So who's driving a caravan?" said Macalvie, taking what looked like a single-lane road between hedges stout as stone walls at a good fifty miles per hour. God help them or anyone coming from the opposite direction.

It was seven in the morning but it looked like dusk — the rain, the ground mist, the dark rock formations rising against the sky. When they got beyond the hedged-in road, Jury saw acres of heather the color of port, crippled trees, the occasional huddled house.

Ashcroft was visible from a turning a half-mile away, standing on its hill, a large and perfectly proportioned house. As they turned into its long, sweeping gravel drive, Jury saw the grounds were partly formal — well-groomed hedges, flower beds — and partly wild, as if the gardener had dropped spade and hoe in the middle of the job.

In front were two police cars.

"Nice little place," said Macalvie, braking hard enough to spit up gravel.

"What the hell do you mean, a *ruse?*"

Detective Inspector Browne looked as if he'd like to be anywhere but where he was now. "Sorry, sir. The little girl, Jessica Ashcroft — or Lady Jessica, I should say, I expect —"

"I don't care what you call her, Browne. Just tell me what's going on."

Eyes averted from Macalvie's, Browne explained. "And by the time we found out, you'd already left Lyme Regis. . . ."

Jessica looked up at the three new ones. She was still in her nightdress, as were the other members of the household. She sat on the couch, ankles crossed, patiently waiting for whatever scolding the new ones had to dish out. There should be enough brains among all of them to find her uncle, she thought. She did not particularly like the look of the copper-haired one who stood with his hands in his trouser pockets and had eyes like torches. The other, taller one had gray eyes and looked, somehow, comfortable. . . .

Macalvie looked over the lot of them. Victoria Gray was sitting patiently enough on the couch facing the girl. The older one was the cook and she wrung her hands. Then there was the rich pastry of a piece named Plunkett. Their backdrop, the drawing room itself, was heavy velvet and brocade, portraits and gilt. No one was hurting for money.

"This," said DI Browne, "is Lady Jessica Mary Allan-Ashcroft."

On facing sofas, Chief Superintendent Macalvie and Jessica Allan-Ashcroft squared off. Jury sat in a heavy brocade chair and Wiggins in a straight one by the fire.

"You can call me Jessica," she said, with extreme largesse.

"Thanks." Macalvie glared at her, took out a pack of gum, and stuffed a stick in his mouth.

"Can I have some?"

Jury was glad to see Macalvie managed to keep from throwing it at her.

They both sat there, taking each other's measure, chewing away.

"Start talking," said Macalvie.

"My uncle's missing."

That statement seemed to bring housekeeper, cook, and governess to the edge of hysteria. Victoria Gray, the most controlled, stepped back from it and said to Macalvie, "Robert Ashcroft. Her uncle. He left several days ago, probably for London, but she's convinced he's missing. It's ridiculous; Mr. Ashcroft goes to London now and again."

Macalvie's eyes snapped from Victoria back to Jessica. He chewed and stared. "You know, there's kind of a difference between an uncle going missing and a friendly call from an ax-murderer. That occur to you?"

Jury broke in. "What makes you think he's missing, Jessica?"

"Because he didn't leave a note and he didn't leave a Valentine present."

"For a box of candy," said Macalvie, "you got half the Devon-Cornwall constabulary running across this godforsaken, bloody moor with some cock-and-bull story about a murderer. You know that, don't you?"

To that deadly voice, Jessie sighed and said, "I'm sorry."

"You're sorry."

She smoothed the skirt of her nightdress, folded her hands, and said gravely, "Yes. I'm sorry you're so disappointed that there wasn't a lot of blood and torn-up bodies and we weren't all murdered, including Henry." She took out her gum, inspected the pink wad, and put it back in her mouth.

Macalvie's eyes were like lasers. He opened his mouth but was interrupted.

"Don't forget about that man that got out of Dartmoor." As if police weren't keeping abreast of the news, she handed Macalvie a neatly folded paper. It contained the clipping that Drucilla had read earlier.

Macalvie tossed the paper aside, angrily. "That *man* was *released* on good behavior. Your behavior I'm not so sure I could say the same about. Not only the Devon-Cornwall police, but the person sitting over there" — and he nodded in

Jury's direction — "just happens to be a Scotland Yard CID superintendent."

"Then why isn't he asking the questions?" Jessica directed her attention to Jury. "My uncle disappeared five days ago, six, counting today." She was pleased the thin one was making notes of what she said. At least *someone* was taking her seriously. "He never forgets any holiday and he always lets me know if he has to go somewhere. Besides that, all of his cars are out there." She pointed in the direction of the stable-yard.

"What do you mean, 'all,' Miss?" asked Wiggins.

"All nine. The Zimmer, the Porsche, the Lotus Elite, the Mini Cooper — that's really mine — the Ferrari, the Jaguar XJ-S that goes from zero to sixty in under seven seconds, the 1967 Maserati, and the Aston Martin." She sat back.

Wiggins cleared his throat. "That's only eight, Miss." He counted with his lips again.

Jury thought Macalvie was going to belt one of them; he wasn't sure which.

Jessica looked for a thoughtful moment at the ceiling. "Did I say the Benz? I don't like it that much."

Wiggins wrote it down. "Your uncle's a collector, is that it?" He wet the tip of his pencil.

"Yes. He's five-feet-eleven with gold hair and light brown eyes." She looked back at Jury. "He's handsome. He took me in when my father died four years ago."

There was a slight laugh from Victoria Gray: "Wasn't it more like your taking *him* in?"

Jury looked more closely at her: good-looking, eyes heavy-lidded, as if she preferred not to have her thoughts read in her eyes. She seemed embarrassed now, having given voice to one of those thoughts. "Pardon me, but I'd like to get dressed." She drew the velvet wrapper more closely around her.

"Go ahead," said Macalvie. "Except for missing uncles there's no reason for us to be here."

Jessie looked around the room. "You're not even going to look for him, are you?"

Jury was impressed with the little girl's conviction that something was really wrong. Her uncle must be a very dependable person. "We will."

Macalvie was standing now, hands in pockets, turning the blowtorch look on Jury. "Isn't there enough on your platter already?"

"I just thought I'd ask Lady Jessica a few questions."

"Hell, ask away. I'm going down to Freddie's. Browne can drop me off and you can bring the car along whenever you're finished fooling around here. Come on, Wiggins. One drink of Freddie's cider and you'll never be sick a day in your life. You'll be paralytic."

Wiggins looked at Jury; Jury nodded. It amused him that Wiggins — or the pharmacy Wiggins carried with him — had become indispensable to Macalvie.

III

There in the drawing room, Jury listened patiently to the fabrication of faithless loves and deaths from broken hearts attributed to her mother. She had gone to a table on which stood some framed pictures and brought back the one of Barbara Allan Ashcroft. The woman in the picture, even squinting and half-blinded by the sun, Jury could see was herself blindingly beautiful. She might indeed have broken many of the hearts Jessica claimed she had.

The second picture was of her father: he was an older and more wasted version of the man in the portrait above the fireplace; a grave illness would explain it.

"She's pretty, isn't she?"

"She's more than pretty. She's quite beautiful. You look like her, you know." The woman was probably in her twenties, at any rate she was a good twenty years younger than her husband. Jury could almost believe the tale of woe and heartbreak Jessica had spun. Unfortunately, though, Jessica suffered from the Scheherazade syndrome. Whenever there came a pause in her tale of gloom and doom and Jury made to get up, Jessie would spin out an even richer thread. Scheherazade or Hephaestus — Jury wasn't sure which. He would start to rise and *plunk*, the golden net would fall and toss him back once more onto the couch. Her contriving the ax-murderer's visit was small potatoes, compared with the tragedy of Barbara Allan. If as many suitors had died for love of Jessica's mother as Jessica would have him believe, the population of London W1, Devon and Chalfont St. Giles would have been considerably diminished. Jessie was careful to assure Jury, however, that her mother would never have deliberately hurt whatever Sweet William happened to be in love with her at a given moment.

Barbara Ashcroft had died a few months after Jessie was born. When her Uncle Robert had gone off to Australia, Jessie had not yet been born. Victoria Gray (according to Jessie) had come to her mother's funeral and, being a cousin, had been urged to stay on by her father. There was an old cook who was especially fond of Lady Ashcroft and who had preferred to leave once she was dead. Thus, Mrs. Mulchop had come on the job afterwards. And so had the string of governesses.

No one in the present household had known Robert Ashcroft before he came back from Australia.

Jessie went on about her father, her uncle, her other relatives (all of whom were very distant). "After the will was read, they kept coming and calling, until Uncle Rob got rid of them."

"Do you know who your family solicitor is, Jessie?" asked Jury. They were out in the stableyard now, behind the house, a handsomely converted stableyard.

"It's Mr. Mack. Or, at least, he's one of them. We have —"

She seemed uncertain as to how much they had. "— trunks full of money. Do you like cars?"

"How long has he been with the family?"

She frowned. "Who?"

"Your solicitor, Mr. Mack."

"Forever. Do you like *cars*?"

He felt an odd presentiment. Wynchcoombe, Clerihew Marsh, Lyme Regis, Dorchester. Only the last was outside a forty-mile radius. But the Ashcroft place was certainly within it. And she was ten years old.

"Yes. I like cars," said Jury.

They had come to the last of the nine — one of Jessie's favorites — the Lotus Elite. "Nineteen fifty-seven," she solemnly pronounced. Then she went on to interweave fact and fiction, using expressions like "stroke dimension" and "wishbone front" with all the assurance of an expert.

It was during this recital that there came a rush of footsteps and raised voices and a man striding across the courtyard toward the old horse-boxes. "Jess! What the devil's going on?"

The look on her face made it clear to Jury that Uncle Robert was no longer missing.

FOURTEEN

H E would have needed no introduction. The way Jessie hurled herself like a discus into his arms would have told Jury that this was Robert Ashcroft.

"But I *did* leave a note," he was saying as Jury walked up. "I slipped it under your door. Who's our visitor?" He looked from Jessie to Jury.

"Scotland Yard." Jury handed Ashcroft his card, smiling to show his was a friendly visit. "It seems Lady Jessica got a little worried and told police you'd gone missing. The Devon police have been and gone."

Ashcroft looked down at his niece, astonished. "Good God, Jess. You called in police —" He looked at Jury and down at Jury's card. "Scotland Yard? I can't believe it."

"Well, I happened to be working on another case and came along with the divisional commander —"

Again, amazement was stamped on Ashcroft's face. "A superintendent and a divisional commander, Jess? Where's the Prime Minister? You left her out? How in the name of heaven did Jess manage to drag you all out here on a missing person case?"

Jessica was studying an interesting cloud formation and saying maybe they should go in as it looked like rain. Inspired by another means of changing the subject, she called for Henry. "Where's Henry? He came out with us. *Henry!*"

The sad face of Henry appeared slowly, rising behind the windscreen of the Ferrari.

"He likes to go for rides," said Jessie, as she pulled away from her uncle and made Henry clamber down from the car.

Out of sight, out of mind, thought Jury, smiling. "Sorry about the police intrusion, Mr. Ashcroft. All a mare's nest. I've been working on a case in Dorchester —"

"I read about it. Terrible."

"What's more terrible is there've been two others since then."

Ashcroft looked at his niece and went a little white. "Children?"

Jury nodded.

Jessica was back with Henry in tow. "One got stuck with a knife and the other one got his head bashed in, or something." She made a dreadful sound, apparently her version of bashing.

"It's nothing to be making light of, Jess," said her uncle, sharply.

"I wasn't. I was just showing you — it happened in the church, too."

Ashcroft looked puzzled. "What church?"

"Over in Wynchcoombe."

Her proximity to murder did not seem to faze her, but Ashcroft looked worried enough as he studied Jury's face for some reassurance. Jury doubted he wanted to go further into details in front of his niece, and said nothing.

Jessie, however, had garnered plenty of details: "It's Drucilla who told me. She likes to read me the worst part of the papers. An ax-murderer got out of the prison in Princetown —"

Jury laughed. "Hold it a minute. The man was *released,* Jessie. There was even some question whether he'd ever done that — business. And he certainly wasn't an 'ax-murderer'; the papers like blood and thunder."

Ashcroft was angry, though not at Jury. "Drucilla's days are numbered. She shouldn't have been reading you that sort of stuff. And didn't you get the candy I paid that stupid bloke she runs about with to deliver?"

"Drucilla said the chocolates *were for her!* She's been stuffing them in till she's bloated."

"I'll see to her. At any rate, I've found you a new governess. This one I think will finally do."

Jury could almost hear the *Oh, no* directed toward her uncle. Beseeching eyes. Down-turned mouth. "But you always let me choose before!"

"I'm sorry, Jess. But they've all turned out to be such a bad lot — well, anyway, this time I advertised in the London papers. That's why I went up to London. You'll like Sara. I'm sure of it. And if you don't —" Ashcroft shrugged. "— she goes. Okay? In the meantime, I think you might want to meet her. She's in the drawing room."

Jessie didn't answer. Her eyes were on the ground

"If there are no further questions, Superintendent — ?"

Jury was fascinated by Jessie's little act. She might have been going to a hanging. "Questions? No, Mr. Ashcroft. No questions." He looked back toward the boxes that housed not horses but cars. "I was wondering, though, if I could have another look at your collection —"

"Certainly. Help yourself."

Jessie held him back, saying, "That's another thing. Why didn't you take one of the cars? Why didn't you drive?"

Ashcroft smoothed back her dark hair. "Because there was an advert in the paper about a Rolls; I was sure I'd buy it and drive it back. But it wasn't what I wanted. And as it turned out, Miss Millar — that's Sara — had her own car. So we drove back."

Looking at Jessie's face, Jury thought the news couldn't have been worse. He only hoped, for the niece's sake, Miss Millar's car was a beat-up Volkswagen.

Jessie and Ashcroft walked off, hand in hand. Jury doubted it would take much time for Jessie to sort out the new tutor.

He walked along the courtyard, looking at each of the expensive automobiles in turn: the Ferrari, the Porsche, the Aston Martin, the incredible Zimmer Golden Spirit (he whistled under his breath), the Mercedes-Benz (that probably didn't get much of a workout), the Jag — there was a fortune here.

His skin prickled. Jury took out his notebook and wrote down the name of the solicitor, Mack. Robert Ashcroft's explanation had been plausible enough: note slipped under the door (that Jury bet had been mistakenly tossed out by a maid); chocolates meant to be delivered by surprise — and clearly were, since Miss Plunkett had been eating them . . .

Yet there was that same reluctance to leave as there was when Jessica had been spinning her stories. He wished he had some legitimate reason for coming back —

He could suggest to Ashcroft that, with a killer loose nearby, his niece might need police protection. But Robert Ashcroft would hire a personal bodyguard and get a matched set of Alsatians if he thought his niece was a target for a killer.

Jury was standing in front of Jessie's car, the Mini Cooper. It might as well have been a police-issue Cortina for all of Jury's interest in cars.

But then he smiled and ground his cigarette out on the stone and left.

V

The Jack and
Hammer

FIFTEEN

An air of somnolence hung over the Jack and Hammer's saloon bar, an air not altogether owing to the fly droning around the black beams overhead, nor to Mrs. Withersby's dozing by the fire, nor to the report of the latest takeover bid of another shipyard, which was what Melrose Plant was reading about in the *Times*. Indeed, the only thing moving — and possibly responsible for the general heaviness — was Lady Ardry's mouth.

"*Gout!* That is ridiculous, Melrose." She addressed the London *Times*, behind which was the face of her nephew. "It most certainly is *not* gout!" Now she addressed the painful foot, elastic-bound and supported by the cricket stool that Mrs. Withersby ordinarily claimed for herself. On this occasion, the usual Withersby enterprise had exchanged it for a double gin, compliments of Melrose Plant, the nephew Lady Ardry was now upbraiding. "And if it *is* gout, *you'd* have it, not I!"

He lowered the paper. "I'd have *your* gout, Agatha? That would be a first in the annals of medicine."

"Please do not try to be witty with *me*, my dear Plant."

"That would be difficult." Melrose turned to the book reviews, having exhausted global conflict.

"What I meant was, as you perfectly well know, that it's *you* who drinks the port, not *I.*" She raised her glass of shooting sherry, toasting her own powers of deduction.

Melrose lowered his *Times* once again and turned his eyes to the beams above, wondering if the fly would fall like a bullet in the vacuum of their conversation. "Gout has many causes, Agatha. Perhaps you have fairy-cake-gout. Who knows but that if you eschew those rich pastries, your foot might become less inflamed, as the condition is not irreversible." He wondered if life were, though, when talking to his aunt. He continued. "Gout comes from the Latin *gutta.* It means 'clot' or 'drop.' Surely, you don't believe that every old pukka sahib drinking port beneath the palms wound up with gout? Gout is caused by uric acid. Sort of thing you get with too many sardines or smelts or offal. You haven't been at the offal again, have you?"

"This is just what I would have expected of you, Plant. No sympathy whatever."

"Then why did you come clumping into the Jack and Hammer on your cane, if you already knew?" Trying to change the subject from gout to books and thinking that Agatha might be interested (by some weird crossover of the stars) in American writers, as she herself was American, Melrose said, "Now, just look at this —"

Look at this might better have been said of the man coming through the Jack and Hammer's door — Long Piddleton's antiques dealer, Marshall Trueblood. Trueblood always managed to appear on any scene like a voyager on the deck of a departing ocean liner, all confetti and colored streamers. Nothing so much resembled one as the purple crepe scarf loosely knotted at his neck and trembling in the same wind that stirred the cape of his cashmere inverness.

Dick Scroggs, the publican, looked up from his paper, spread out on the bar, and with that welcome reserved for regulars said, "Close the bleedin' door, mate." He then returned to his paper.

"My *dear* Scroggs. How can you be so churlish when trade is this good? There are at least three — well two and a half" (he corrected himself, looking at Mrs. Withersby) "— customers. Plant, Agatha." He unwhirled his handsome coat and took a seat as close to Lady Ardry's lame foot as would allow for a little bit of pain.

She said *ouch* and glared at Trueblood, whom she loathed only slightly less than Mrs. Withersby. Trueblood, after all, had money. Not as much as her nephew, but money nonetheless.

Trueblood called to the publican for drinks all around, and included Mrs. Withersby with a helping of gin-and-it. He offered his Balkan Sobranies, lit up a lavender one (in tune with his scarf), and brushed a mite of cigarette coal from his sea-green shirt. Trueblood was the jewel in the crown of Long Piddleton, a dazzling little collection of cottages and shops in the hills of Northamptonshire. Scroggs brought the drinks and Trueblood asked Plant what he was so deep into reading about.

"Book reviews."

"How lovely. Anything useful?"

Trueblood, though certainly no tightwad, couldn't help but think of everything in terms of usury.

"I was going to read this review to Agatha, since she's American —"

"I *do* wish you would stop referring to me in that way, Plant." Tenderly she touched the bandage like a newborn baby's cheek. "You always seem to forget that I married your uncle, and that —"

She was always shaking relatives from his family tree, as if Melrose couldn't remember them on his own. He ignored her. "Listen. 'This tone of easy superiority can sometimes be grating, primarily because it is symptomatic of a culture in its imperial phase —' "

"Who are they reviewing?" asked Trueblood. "Gunga Din?"

"No. It's this collection of essays by John Updike. But what in hell does it mean? Even leaving off the 'imperial phase' stuff — I mean the U.S. And just what is Updike's 'easy superiority'?"

"It's probably what Withers has." Trueblood called over to Cinders-by-the-ashes. "Withers, old trout! Another gin-and-it?"

Mrs. Withersby spat in the fire at the same time she hobbled over to the bar for a refill.

Trueblood went on. "No, I'd say easy superiority is what Franco Giopinno has. Vivian's slippery Italian."

Vivian Rivington, a long-standing and (in some minds) beautiful friend, was off in Italy visiting her "slippery Italian."

"Ah, yes. That's it precisely," continued Trueblood, marveling yet once again at himself. "Do you suppose she's gone to Venice to break it off or put it on — oh, sorry, old trout —" He turned to Agatha with innocent eyes. "That did sound a bit off-color."

"You needn't apologize to *me*, Mr. Trueblood! I'm sure I can put it on with the best of them."

Trueblood and Melrose exchanged glances.

"But if she thinks herself a woman of such superiority —"

"Uh-uh. *Easy* superiority," Trueblood said. "It's like easy virtue. What do you think, Melrose? I know how fond you are of Viv-viv."

It was deliberate. It always was with Trueblood when Lady Ardry was around. Melrose knew she would gladly have given Trueblood a crack with her cane, had it not been more important to divert Plant's attention away from Vivian into other and less attractive quarters.

"*I* find the review extremely un-American."

"Well, it's certainly anti-Updike," said Melrose. "'An American confidence which can treat the whole world as a suitable province for its judgments.'" He could only shake his head. "For the British to talk imperialism ... Cheap shot."

The only cheap shot Agatha was concerned about was where her next shooting sherry was coming from.

"And here's another American writer being gunned down. She's described as writing a book 'ladylike in an American way.' That only makes me want to meet American ladies, to find out in what way they're so differently ladylike." Melrose looked at Trueblood, but doubted he'd have much to offer on that point.

"As far as I am concerned," said Agatha, "I mean to stay right here in dear old England." She patted her upraised ankle. "You will never get *me* back to the United States."

That was a good reason for a mass exodus, thought Melrose. But, then, why *should* she go back to the States? She had everything here she could ever want. Unfortunately for her, all of it was up at Ardry End — the crystal, the Queen Anne furniture, the servants, grounds and jewels. . . . Well, perhaps not *all* of the jewels, for Melrose noticed that riding on her bosom this afternoon was a delicately chased silver brooch he had last seen in his mother's possession. The Countess of Caverness had been dead for a number of years; his aunt seemed set on slipping into her shoes, even though Agatha was not, properly speaking, a Lady in any sense of the term. She had been married to Melrose's uncle — the Honorable Robert Ardry. Agatha had decided to let the dead bury the dead, but not the title, and had long since wedded herself instead to the cake stand and the shooting sherry.

"I cannot imagine," said Melrose, "one's giving up America to come live in a country of amateurs."

Trueblood raised an eyebrow at that. "And do you include

retreaders of furniture in that category?" His description of himself and his antiques was hardly accurate.

Agatha sighed loudly. "I don't know what you're talking about, Plant."

She seldom did. It inspired Melrose to dip into further shallows of conversation, even if it was like wasting a good fly on a dead fish. "I am referring to amateur shopkeepers, amateur publicans, amateur politicians, amateur butchers —"

Lady Ardry sat up a bit too sharply and winced with pain. It was all right for Melrose to toy with prime ministers, but certainly not with the source of her daily chop. "Amateur butchers! You'd insult Mr. Greeley — after that magnificent joint we had just last evening —?"

"I'm not insulting Mr. Greeley's joints. But he's back there with hatchets and cleavers and saws, for all I know." Perhaps it was this reference in the paper to the release of a prisoner from Dartmoor who had been dubbed the "ax-murderer" that had allowed him to see Mr. Greeley in that light.

"Melrose! You're putting me off my sherry."

Melrose continued reading. It was possible to talk to Agatha and read simultaneously. "What I'm talking about is this: I bet you don't find American butchers greeting their customers while wearing blood-smeared aprons with knives in their hands. Everytime I see your Mr. Greeley I'm reminded of the *Texas Chain Saw Murders* or whatever that execrable film was we saw on ITV. And there's another category, too — amateur criminals. You've got — meaning America has, or had — Al Capone and Scarface and the Godfather and Richard Nixon. All we've got is Brixton and the IRA."

"I must say, old bean," said Marshall Trueblood, "that's hardly a compliment to the U.S.A."

"Not meant to be. I'm merely saying that when the Americans do something — at least the professional criminals, it's a bang-up job. Not slapdash, like most of ours."

"You're mad as a hatter, Melrose. Right round the twist.

I'd like another drink, if you would be so kind." Agatha was not in the habit of inspecting her bread closely to see on which side it was buttered.

Melrose continued with his thesis. "Don't you remember John McVicar, who escaped from Durham? That's a high-security lockup, just like Dartmoor. No one had done it before —"

"Which merely disproves your point, old chap." Trueblood rose to get the drinks, and Mrs. Withersby snapped to attention.

"No, it doesn't. Two of them got out. One broke his ankle going over the wall or something and the plan for the pickup had to be dished. Well, there goes John into the Wear or the Tyne — whichever river — and he swims for it. But now he's got the problem of making contact with his friends on the outside. Guess how he does it?"

Agatha sighed even more loudly because Melrose was keeping Trueblood away from the bar. "Can't imagine," said Trueblood.

"Goes into a public call box. I mean, for God's sakes, can you imagine Capone or Scarface in a phone booth searching for a ten-p piece — ?"

Scroggs interrupted by calling from the bar, "Phone for you, M'lord." Dick Scroggs had never been able to work his mind round to Melrose Plant's having given up his title.

"A call?" said Agatha. "Here? Who would be calling you at the Jack and Hammer? I find that odd. . . ." She kept on casting about for reasons all the time Melrose was making his way to the phone on the other side of the bar.

It was Ruthven, his butler. Melrose was so mystified by the message that Ruthven had to convince him that, Yes, those were Superintendent Jury's directions. He would very much appreciate Lord Ardry's motoring to Dartmoor in his Silver Ghost — "He was very specific on that point, My Lord." Superintendent Jury had left clear instructions as to what he would like Lord Ardry to do.

"Yes, all right," said Melrose. "Yes, yes, yes, Ruthven. Thank you." Melrose hung up.

His friend Jury might have asked for some odd things over the years of their acquaintance, but why would he want an earl with a Silver Ghost?

VI

The End of
the Tunnel

SIXTEEN

JESSICA stood in the doorway of the drawing room that morning, refusing to put her foot over the sill, as if she hoped that might spirit away the person to whom she was being introduced. She wouldn't look up and she wouldn't come forward despite her uncle's growing impatience. It was because she knew what she'd see.

The Amiable Amy.

In that wonderful catchall tone that Uncle Rob could use when he was cross with her, yet understood her dilemma (a common occurrence in the household), he said, "Miss Millar will think you are determined always to address her from the other side of the room, Jess."

With daggers in her eyes, she looked at her uncle, and then quickly down again lest the eyes might meet Miss Millar's.

Now it was Miss Millar's voice — amiable as could be — saying, "I can remember once having to meet a new teacher. I can remember being very shy of her."

Shy? *Shy?* Jessica Mary Allan-Ashcroft? Never in her life — or, at least, in the life she had led after Uncle Robert had come along — had Jessie been called "shy." Her face colored with rage, which only made her more furious because now it would be taken as proof of her being shy.

"Come on, Jess," said her uncle. Seldom could she remember his sounding as if Jessie's behavior were an embarrassment to him. Now, that's just how he sounded.

Henry, hearing the *Come on*, drifted out of his light doze, even though he was on his feet.

"Not you," she murmured, giving him a little kick.

The amiable voice continued: "Well, then, perhaps we can talk at luncheon. Or dinner." Now there was amusement in the voice. "Breakfast? Though I might not last that long. . . ."

That was smart of the new governess. It was as if she were trying to make light of what even Jessie knew to be perfectly odious behavior on her own part. Of course, the Amiable Amy would have to have a sense of humor. Because Uncle Rob had a smashing sense of humor, and Jessie knew humor would make up for all other sorts of defects. Except, perhaps, absolute ugliness. If Amy looked like an ogre or gnome . . . Jessie hazarded a quick glance upward. The case was hopeless. The Amiable Amy was almost *pretty*. Hopeless. She also had patience. Patience on a monument, she was. Jessie knew a lot of Shakespeare because the Mad Margaret had shoveled it — play after play of it — down her throat, Margaret acting out scenes and bawling soliloquies. Margaret had always wanted to be an actress. She was good at Lady Macbeth.

"Jess." There was Uncle Rob again, being beastly. "What *are* you doing, standing there like a statue and wringing your hands?"

Eyes closed, Jessie said, "Not *wringing*. I'm *washing* them. I must wash my hands. Nothing will make them come clean. They're incar——" She couldn't remember that word. It was something like carburetor.

Uncle Robert was actually beginning to sound concerned. "Jessie. Are you ill? What's the matter?" He laughed uncertainly. "You seem to have gone a little mad."

Quite. She smiled to herself and turned and ran from the room.

Since the exit included no *Come on, Henry,* Henry continued to doze in the doorway.

SEVENTEEN

"So here's what happened," said Macalvie. They were sitting in the mobile unit in Wynchcoombe, Macalvie having cleared the place of the sergeant manning the telecom system, three constables going in and out, and TDC Coogan. The only person (besides Jury and Wiggins) who had held his ground was Detective Inspector Neal, calmly observing Macalvie over the rim of his coffee cup.

"You've solved it, Macalvie?" Neal's tone was wry. "I sure as hell hope so. Because I don't seem to be getting anywhere. Our chief constable is a little upset. He keeps getting these calls from frightened parents."

Macalvie leaned back in his chair, hands laced behind his head. He gave Neal his laser-look. "That's too bad. Give Dorset my blessing and ask your chief if he'll grant me another twenty-four hours."

Neal smiled and dumped the rest of his coffee in the sink. "I'll do it straightaway. In the meantime, I better go back and look for the Riley boy's killer. Don't you think?"

Solemnly, Macalvie nodded. "It'd be a great kindness to Dorset police."

Neal left, shaking his head.

Macalvie started talking as if it hadn't been Neal, but Neal's wraith that had just floated out the door, part of a spirit-world set to drive him mad, since the forces of the real world couldn't dent him.

"Take the name of the pub where this string of killings started, the Five Alls: the sign is usually divided so you see these five figures representing authority. 'I pray for all' — that'd be a priest or other symbol of the church; 'I plead for all' — barrister or solicitor; 'I fight for all' — military, right? 'I rule all' — a lot of positions fit that; and 'I take all.' Interesting, that figure. Sometimes the Five Alls sign says, 'I pay for all,' meaning king, queen, and country. Other times the fifth figure is John Bull, who 'pays for all.' But in our Dorchester Five Alls, the fifth figure is the Devil, who 'takes all.' Like lives. Now, we've got George-bloody-Thorne, solicitor; we've got Davey White's granddad, vicar —"

Wiggins interrupted. "But you're forgetting Simon Riley's father is only a butcher."

Macalvie smiled slightly. "True, but his wife's got some family connection with a Q.C. who's running for Parliament — 'I rule for all,' in other words. That's two figures left: the soldier and the Devil. The Devil's the killer. So that leaves one more murder." He looked at Jury. "Your expression tells me you don't like my theory. Disaster." Macalvie held out his hand to Wiggins, who rolled a lozenge into it. "I'm sure you noticed the portrait of Jessica Ashcroft's father."

"Of course. He was a Grenadier. Military." Macalvie opened the top drawer of a desk and took out a pint of whiskey and a smudged glass. "I'm going to quit this lousy job, I swear to God. Go to America. The booze is cheaper." He looked up at the ceiling as if the geography of the United States were etched there, uncapped the bottle, took a drink, and handed the glass to Wiggins.

"We might have come to the same conclusion by different routes," said Jury. "That is, if you're thinking of Jessica Ashcroft."

"Yeah. I'm also thinking of Sam Waterhouse. He sat in a cell for nearly nineteen years, knowing he was railroaded." Macalvie shook his head. "I still say he's not the type. He wasn't once and he *still* isn't. Are you reading your fortune in the bottom of that glass, Wiggins, or are you going to pass it along?"

"Waterhouse would be a dead cert, given *your* reasoning. Hatred of authority. And he got out just before these murders were committed."

Macalvie lapped his hands round the glass and studied the ceiling. "I still don't think it's Sam."

"What about Robert Ashcroft?"

Macalvie stopped looking at the ceiling and took his feet off his desk. "Meaning?"

"Four million pounds. And being gone just over the days of the murders. No one in the present Ashcroft household had ever seen him before he returned from Australia. I'm going up to London to talk to the Ashcroft solicitor. But even if Ashcroft *is* the real brother, there's still —"

Macalvie interrupted. "The Campbell Soup Kid's money. Right?"

Jury nodded.

"Then why the other killings? A blind?"

Jury nodded again.

Macalvie shook his head as if he were trying to clear it, poured some more whiskey in the glass and handed it to Jury. "What's his story about taking BritRail to London?"

"That he thought he'd be buying a Roller advertised in the *Times.*"

"I'll have somebody checking the paper on that one, to see if there *was* a car. And check to see if Ashcroft really went to see it. But let's assume — just for the sake of the argument —"

"I'm not trying to argue, Macalvie." Jury handed the whiskey glass to Wiggins, knowing he wouldn't drink from the same ditch. "I just think Jessica Ashcroft's in trouble."

Macalvie went on as if Jury hadn't interrupted. "— that Ashcroft's guilty. Ask again — why didn't he drive up to London? He stayed at the Ritz. The doorman would have noticed any of those cars of Ashcroft coming in and out. He couldn't have used his own cars. They'd attract too much attention. It's got to be either train, bus, rented car. No, renting's too risky. Probably train. Early morning train from Exeter to London on the tenth, and he has a talk with the stationmaster to make sure he's remembered *leaving* the area. He checks into the Ritz. Train back to Dorchester — it's only a three-hour trip—six hours coming and going. Or he could even have got off in Dorchester, killed the Riley boy, then gone on to London. On the twelfth, to Waterloo Station, late night train to Exeter — no, not Exeter. The stationmaster might remember him. Axminster. What about Axminster?"

Wiggins shook his head. "Why would he go to all of that trouble? Going back and forth? If he wants to put us on the trail of a psychopath — ?"

"Because he's got to be *out* of the area the killings are done in," said Macalvie.

"Then what does he do," said Jury, "after he gets off your Axminster train? He can't *walk* to Wynchcoombe. How does he get there? And how does he get to Lyme Regis?"

"Not the train, then. So he doesn't rent a car. He *buys* one in London. Something fast and pricey that's already M.O.T.'d. Buys it from one of the sleazy grafters all over London. They don't give a damn what name you tell them. That gives Ashcroft the thirteenth to do his interviewing of tutors and allows her to pack up and they go back to Ashcroft on the fifteenth." He looked at Jury. "So what do you think?"

"Do you care?"

"Not particularly. We'll circulate pictures round the used-car lots. Pictures. But I don't want to breath on Ashcroft hard enough to make him suspicious." Jury's theory had now become his. "I can't send a police photographer."

"We've got a photographer," said Jury.

Macalvie frowned. "Like who?"

"Molly Singer."

Macalvie smiled. "You mean Mary Mulvanney." He sat back and put his feet on his desk.

"Okay, just for the sake of argument, I'll go along with you. Let's say she *is* Mary Mulvanney. Given Sam Waterhouse, given Angela Thorne's father, that certainly adds up to a lot of coincidences. Too many. There's a connection between the murders. The old one and these new ones. The same theory that applies to Waterhouse might apply to her. Revenge. Though the killing of the Riley boy and Davey White isn't clear. Anyway, we get Molly into Ashcroft as a photographer for some classy magazine about cars or the country gentleman. We can certainly work up some bona fides."

Macalvie took his feet off the desk and frowned. "Jury, you're saying you want to put your chief suspect in the *same house* with Jessica Ashcroft?"

"Who says she's my 'chief suspect'? And what about Waterhouse? Anyway, Jessica's living there right now with another suspect. Her uncle. If Molly Singer were guilty, she'd hardly try anything in the house on a photography assignment."

"Mary Mulvanney." From his wallet, Macalvie drew a snapshot. It was a smiling trio of a woman, a little girl, and an older girl with pale skin and dark hair who was the smiling center of the three.

Jury shook his head. "I don't see any more resemblance to Molly Singer than to any dark-haired girl."

Macalvie returned the picture to his wallet.

That's what got Jury. He'd been carrying it around for twenty years. "You'll never get over that fifteen-year-old kid walking into your office and telling you the law's scum, police are scum, and especially *you're* scum. She really got to you, didn't she?"

Macalvie didn't answer for a moment. "No, Jury. She really got to *you*. Let's go talk to her, if that's the only way to convince you who she is."

"A little browbeating?"

"Who, *me?*"

"Just let me handle the photography business, will you? After a chat with you she might not feel like cooperating with police."

II

Macalvie had made himself at home in the chair by the fire, having picked up the black cat and dumped it on the floor. The cat sat like lead at his feet, its tail twitching.

They had appeared unannounced, Macalvie overriding Jury's objections. It had taken enough persuasion on Jury's part to keep the chief superintendent from dragging Molly Singer into the Lyme Regis station.

"I don't know what you're talking about," said Molly, looking from Macalvie to Jury.

"The hell you don't," Macalvie said, working the old Macalvie magic. "Twenty years ago your mother, Rose, was murdered in a little place called Clerihew Marsh —"

"I've never heard of it," said Molly.

"In Dartmoor, maybe forty miles from here."

Her face was a mask, unreadable; her body rigid, untouchable. But the emotion she was holding back seemed forcibly to spread through the room. Jury felt simultaneously drawn to her and held off.

What interested him was that Macalvie seemed totally unaffected. It wasn't that he was an unfeeling man; he just didn't seem bothered by the electricity in the air.

"Would you like to see my birth certificate to prove who I am?"

"Love to." He popped a hard candy in his mouth and leaned toward her. "Papers don't mean sod-all. You could bring in the priest who officiated at your baptism and all the rest you've made your weekly confession to — you *are* a Catholic, I suppose — and it wouldn't matter. You're still Mary Mulvanney. What the hell are you doing in Lyme?"

"Must I get a solicitor?"

Macalvie smiled slightly. "Of course *Singer* could be your married name. Is it?"

"No."

"Why don't you finish telling us just what happened in Clerihew?"

The question surprised Jury. It clearly surprised Molly Singer. And as he asked the question, he had taken the snapshot from his wallet and handed it to her.

She wouldn't take it, so he dropped it in her lap.

"I don't know what you're talking about."

"You really overwork that line, you know?"

Molly looked at Jury almost hopefully, as if he might untangle the web Macalvie was weaving. Jury said nothing, even though, strictly speaking, he had precedence. This was Dorset, not Devon. But there was a chemistry in the room, a delicate balance that he might upset if he intervened.

"Sam Waterhouse is out — but I expect you read about that."

"I've never heard of him." Her voice was flat; her expression bland.

Macalvie had played two aces in a row right off the bottom of the deck — showing her that picture and then suddenly bringing up Sam Waterhouse. Macalvie, for all of his surprises, didn't use cheap ones. He grew serious. Unless that too was a trick. Maybe Macalvie's pack didn't have a bottom. "Let's go over that story of what happened on the Cobb again."

Molly Singer merely shook her head. Still she hadn't touched the picture. "Why? You wouldn't believe it."

He slid down in the chair, crossed one leg over the other, and said, "You'd be surprised." He sounded almost friendly.

She told him. It was the same story she'd told Jury. And she had no explanation. Impulse, she said. To Jury, her story had the form of a dream . . . this woman out on those rocks, finding a dead child, carrying back the dog . . .

He saw Macalvie look at him, reading the expression. His smile was taut and his message clear: *Minder.*

Molly was talking again: "It's the truth, what I told you. I know you don't have sympathy for what might loosely be called 'neurosis' —"

"Try me."

He sounded perfectly sincere. But what did that mean? "When you walked into the hotel dining room, you recognized me, didn't you?"

"I never saw you before that day," she said.

"Well, I sure as hell knew you: the kid who walked into my office twenty years ago and took the place to pieces. You've got to watch that temper, Mary — excuse me, *Molly*—or someday you'll wind up killing somebody."

She stared at him. "So now I'm the chief suspect." She looked down at the picture and shook her head. "It's a poor picture. How could anyone say this girl and I are the same person?"

"I'm not going by the picture and you damned well know it." He reached out his hand for the snapshot.

"What motive would I ever have for killing Angela Thorne?"

"I'm no psychiatrist —"

Bitterly, she said, "That's obvious."

"—but I imagine it'd be very hard to think of your baby sister writing on the wall in her mother's blood. Hard going to that nut-house and seeing her catatonic. And what you screamed at me twenty years ago was that no matter how long it took you'd get your revenge — against police, judges, God — anything responsible for not finding the real killer. Sam Waterhouse was a friend of yours. And you wouldn't look kindly on anyone who helped put him away. George Thorne. The kid's father."

Her face was blank. "I don't know her father *or* what he does or did. You're just determined to make a case up out of whole cloth —"

"The cloth's already cut to fit you, Mary."

She glared at him.

"Circumstantial evidence alone —" said Macalvie.

"It would have been pretty stupid of me, then, to leave my cape and bring the dog back."

"True. I haven't worked that out yet." There seemed to be no doubt in his mind that he would. "Like I say, I'm no psychiatrist."

Molly Singer got up. "And I'm not Mary Mulvanney."

As Macalvie rose, the black cat's tail twitched again, the inverted triangles of its pupils glaring up at him as if to ask, *What fresh hell can this be?*

EIGHTEEN

"EAT your soldiers, Jess."

Robert Ashcroft spoke absently from behind his newspaper. At the breakfast table now sat three where two had been perfectly comfortable before.

"I don't like my toast cut in strips," said Jessie, fingering a page of one of the books she had brought to the table.

Uncle Rob looked up from his paper. "Since when?"

"I don't like my egg topped, either. I like to peel it." Casually, she turned a page of *Rebecca*.

Sara Millar, the third of their party, cocked her head. She was sitting with her back to the window, and the morning light made her pale hair glow.

(*Bleached*, thought Jessie.)

"I'm sorry, Jessica. I guess I just assumed ..." The quiet voice trailed off. The Selfless Sara had undertaken the job of fixing Jessie's breakfast, thereby relieving the underworked Mrs. Mulchop of yet another chore.

"You're still angry with me, aren't you?" Robert Ashcroft looked unhappy.

Jess was sorry for the hurt look on his face and pained because she was its cause. But this was going to be a battle of wits, make no mistake. Thus she must harden her heart. She simply shrugged her indifference.

Of course, that worried her uncle more. "You're acting awfully —"

Sara Millar interrupted, thereby cleverly deflecting the thrust of Robert's words. "What are you reading, Jessie?"

She was clearly determined to be nice as ninepence. "*Rebecca* and *Jane Eyre*." Jess looked Sara straight in the eye. Sara had nice eyes, widely spaced and the same bluish-gray of the suit she had worn yesterday. The eyes were set in just the face that Jessie would have expected: clear-skinned and, if not absolutely *pretty*, it was far from plain, framed as it was by that ash-blond hair. Round her hair was a dusty-rose band that matched her jumper. All of her clothes (Jessie bet) would have that dusty, subdued look — colors muted, makeup understated, just that bare hint of lipstick. The metamorphosis would come later, after she got her claws into Uncle Robert. Then would come trailing the plumy gowns, waterfalls of jewels (Barbara Allan's emeralds, maybe?), the blond hair coiled but with little tendrils struggling free as Sultry Sara swept down Ashcroft's magnificent staircase.

But as for now, Sara Millar was perfectly content to let her beauty lie skin deep.

She had been talking about the books during Jess's ruminations over her transformation: ". . . two of my favorites," said the Selfless Sara.

Jess looked up from the book she was only pretending to read. Uncle Robert had once told her it was rude to read in others' company, but she had merely taken him to task about his morning paper. Jessie was not disposed to bring books to the table, anyway, before now.

"Two of my favorites." Sara would have said that if Jess had brought *Beano* and *Chips and Whizzer* along.

Sara quoted, " 'Last night I dreamed I was at Manderley

again . . . , ' " and she had the nerve to look around the dining room as if Ashcroft might give Manderley a run for its money. "Isn't that a smashing line? I only wish I could write one a quarter as good."

Robert Ashcroft looked at her, seeming pleased. "Do you write, then?"

Sara Miller laughed. "Nothing you'd want to read, I'm sure."

Jessie glared. If she was dreaming of Manderley, why didn't she go back to it? She gave a little kick under the table.

Sara lurched slightly. "What's that?"

Uncle Rob pulled up the tablecloth. "What's Henry doing there? Get him out, Jess."

"It's all right," said Sara, recovering quickly from the paw that had hit her silk-stockinged leg. "I was just surprised. Hullo, Henry."

Jessie watched the traitor Henry burrowing out and accepting a head-rub, all uncaring of the knives grinding in his mistress's mind. "May I be excused?" she asked in a determinedly polite manner.

"To go where?" asked Uncle Rob. "You have to begin lessons."

A look passed between Sara and Uncle Rob. Jessie could barely control her rage. But the Mad Margaret had taught her a lot about control. *"No, no, no, my dahling, No! You don't scream the line out — 'Not all the perfumes of Arabia can ever make this little hand clean.' "*

"I'm going to sit on the wall."

"The wall?" Sara looked puzzled.

"Around the *grounds*," Jess answered, in a tone that suggested Sara must be a bit dim if she didn't know grounds had walls. "I like to sit and look way off at the prison. Where the ax-murderer escaped from."

"Jess, for the umpteenth time, no one *escaped*."

She shrugged as if that made no difference. "Anyway, what

about the murders?" This question was directed to Sara Millar. Jess hoped it might take the place of Rochester's crazy wife.

"Jessie, you oughtn't to be afraid —" Jessie's look stopped Sara.

Afraid? Jess wasn't afraid of anything except her uncle's getting married. With her two books clutched to her chest — and wishing Mrs. Mulchop would wear black and give Sara Millar evil looks, just as Mrs. Danvers did the mouse that married de Winter, she started toward the door.

Victoria Gray was coming in, dressed for riding.

The good-mornings were spoken. Victoria was welcome to share the table, but she stood instead at the sideboard, helping herself to coffee from the silver pot. Since Sara had turned back to her own coffee, she didn't see that dagger-like look that Victoria Gray planted in her back. Jess glanced from the one woman to the other. Although Victoria was better-looking, she was old. At least, nearly as old as Uncle Rob. Selfless Sara was young and dewy, maybe just the age of de Winter's mousy wife.

"Well, I'm off," said Victoria. "Do you ride?" she asked Sara, without enthusiasm.

"A little," Sara said, smiling.

Like she wrote. Probably she was the Brontë sisters and Dick Francis all rolled into one.

II

Don't talk to strangers, Jess, Uncle Robert had cautioned her. As if whole platoons of strangers were walking by the wall trying to engage her in conversation.

She was sitting on the part of the wall that abutted onto one of the end posts that formed Ashcroft's entrance to its long, tree-lined driveway, like a double-barricade against the drive's low, stone wall. On the post was a simple bronze plaque, saying ASHCROFT. Jess often sat here, hoping she'd see something interesting on the road, but she never saw anything except the occasional car or a drover with a bunch of sheep.

It was too high for Henry to clamber up, and she wasn't going to help him because he was doing penance for that head-rub he'd allowed Sara to give him. Henry didn't seem aware he was doing penance; his position was, as usual, prone.

The full horror of her situation was beginning to wash over Jess. Sara Millar had been sitting at breakfast as if she belonged there just as much as the egg cups and the teapot and the toast. A familiar fixture. Yet, there had been no hint at all of her having "taken over." She was merely — at ease.

Jess hit at the stone with her spanner and crumbled a bit of it that drifted dust down onto Henry. He didn't care. No one . . . What was that?

Down the road to her right a car was coming, coming very slowly. Probably tourists limping along, taking their time. Then her eyes opened wide. *What* a car! It was long, elegant — a classic. And it seemed to be in some sort of trouble.

The automobile drew abreast of her and stopped. The driver rolled down the window. "I beg your pardon. You wouldn't know of a garage around here?"

Jessie hopped from the wall and strolled over to the white car with its glistening finish. A dozen coats of lacquer, she bet. Red leather interior. And the winged hood ornament of a Rolls-Royce. She sighed. "No, there's nothing for miles and miles. What do you want one for?"

He smiled. If he was the ax-murderer, he was certainly a good-looking one. Green eyes and sort of straw-colored hair. "Something's wrong. It keeps cutting off —" On cue, the chariot of fire cut off.

"Let's have a look under the bonnet."

He laughed. "I'm not much of a mechanic." He got out.

Jessie squinted up at him. Rich. Good-looking and rich. She took the spanner from her pocket. "I am." She gestured with the spanner, a plan forming in her mind. Where Jessica's thoughts darted, lightning often followed.

Removing his driving gloves, he looked hopefully toward the long tunnel of trees. "Perhaps up there, at the house —"

"Open the bonnet."

III

The moment he saw her sitting on the wall, Melrose Plant swore. If there was one thing he didn't need at this juncture, it was this child. He knew about her; he knew about each member of the household, since Jury had given him details over the telephone. He just hadn't expected her to turn up in dirty overalls with a spanner in her hand.

The plan to get the Silver Ghost just far enough up the drive looked about to be scotched by Jessica Ashcroft. It had been Melrose's intention to let the Rolls rest peacefully on the Ashcroft drive so that he could walk to the house and summon Robert Ashcroft to the rescue. That *was* the plan.

And now here was this ten- or eleven-year-old with black hair and bangs and big brown eyes, with a damned spanner in her hand and a threat in her voice. She stood there, solid as the wall, obviously not about to make a spritely run to summon her elders and betters. He'd have to humor her.

Bonnet up, the two of them peered inside. She did a little clinking about with the spanner and, for one ghastly moment, Melrose was afraid that here might be some mechanical wizard, some garage-prodigy who'd *fix* the damned car. Ah, but she couldn't. Not unless she had a fan belt (which he had removed a quarter of a mile back) to a Rolls in her pocket.

"Look, I wish you wouldn't go banging that thing about. I mean, the old Roller can't take too much of a beating."

She got her head out from under the bonnet and heaved a

sigh. "Probably the carburetor. Only, I can't see why — not on a Rolls-Royce."

"Nothing's perfect."

Her eyes widened. "*That* is." She pointed the spanner at the car.

"Do you think the people in that house up there would just let me pull into the driveway and use the telephone? I think I can get it started again."

Her smile absolutely transformed the sullen little face that had glared from the wall. "I'm *sure* they would. It's *our* house. And my uncle knows lots about cars. He has nine, but not a Rolls-Royce."

"Nine! Imagine that!"

"I don't have to," she said, squinting up at him as if he might be a bit dim. But the tune changed again after she'd run behind the wall and come back with the strangest-looking animal Melrose had ever seen — a dog, he supposed. Though he wouldn't swear to it. "Do you mind if Henry sits with me? You won't get anything dirty, will you, Henry?" she fluted to the odd assortment of laps of skin. It sat on the seat like a wrinkled stump.

She got in; Melrose got in and turned the key. "That's an incredible dog you've got. Isn't it a Shar-pei?"

"Oh, it's only a stray. It might be Chinese." She glanced at Melrose. "It's got green eyes."

The engine turned over and Melrose said, "I can't see its eyes."

She sighed. "No one can."

Melrose got the Silver Ghost partway up the drive before it stopped.

"Don't worry," said Jessica. "My uncle can fix it. Unless he has to send to Exeter for parts. Come on, Henry!" The dog clambered down. "If he does, it'll take a couple of days, I expect." The expectation made her smile.

The house was magnificent — Palladian, made of Portland stone. Must be spare rooms all over. "Look, now. I don't want to put your uncle to any trouble."

Her answer rang with sincerity. "You won't! Really! My name's Jessie Ashcroft. What's yours?" And then she was skipping backwards like any ordinary ten-year-old. Happy, carefree.

"My name's Plant. The family name, that is." This was the part Melrose abhorred.

She stopped dead. "You mean you've got a title?"

Jessica Ashcroft would know about titles, given that her father had had one.

"Well, yes. Yes, as a matter of fact. Earl of Caverness."

Her eyes widened. "My *father* was an earl." And then her glance was a little wary. "I guess because you're expected home you're going to have to ring up the countess?"

"No. There is no Countess of Caverness. I'm not married, you see."

She saw. Her smile beamed at him again. As they ascended the broad steps of Ashcroft, she told him about her uncle and Mrs. Mulchop and Victoria Gray and her new governess, Miss Millar.

And she continued to paint the canvas of Sara Millar in the most astonishing colors. She was beautiful, beneficent, agreeable . . .

Melrose noticed Henry was not with them.

"Oh, him?" Jessie said to his question. "He likes to sleep in cars; he's probably climbed back in. Never mind him." And she put the last dab of color to the portrait of Miss Millar by saying, "Honestly, she's almost saintly."

IV

"Wonderful," said Robert Ashcroft, his head half-buried under the bonnet of the Rolls-Royce. "Absolutely terrific. Just look at the way . . ."

Thus had Mr. Ashcroft gone on, while Melrose shifted from one foot to another, bored to tears with the lesson he was getting in auto-mechanics.

"It's only the fan belt. Can't imagine one simply slipping off. But we can get one from London."

Jessie beamed up at Melrose.

"So please," said Ashcroft, "be my guest, won't you?"

"Oh. But I couldn't *possibly* impose . . ."

No one seemed to notice Plant was a few steps ahead of them as they started toward the house again.

NINETEEN

WHY Sara Millar had been presented by Jessica Ashcroft as the well-wrought urn round which played all the lively virtues, Melrose could not imagine.

Sara Millar was not overly smooth, often clever in her conversation, and very nearly pretty. She seemed to just miss being all or any of those things completely. She wasn't so much the urn, but a very mixed bouquet done up quickly for the occasion. Melrose thought she might be somewhat too much of a soft touch for the likes of Lady Jessica. But then he thought he detected in Miss Millar's velvet glove something of an iron hand. He doubted that Jessica would welcome anyone's telling her what to do.

Other, that is, than her uncle, whom she clearly adored. The feeling seemed to be mutual: Robert Ashcroft thought the world of his niece.

But, then, if one is sitting next to four million pounds, one might not find it difficult to give it a loving pat on the head. Cynical of him. Yet, he had been sent here to be cynical — or, at least, objective. Who was it in the household Jury suspected if not Ashcroft himself? It was too bad that the man was so likable. He was unpretentious and hospitable, not particularly impressed by Melrose's titles. Yet Jury told him to trot out the whole batch of them. Agatha was missing a rare treat in not hearing all of that Earl of Caverness; Viscount of Nitherwold, Ross and Cromarty; Baron Mountardry stuff dragged out.

The introductions were handed round in the drawing room during a pleasant hour set aside for cocktails. There was Victoria Gray, who did not fit at all the role of housekeeper-secretary. In her background were culture and breeding, more so than in Sara Millar's. Victoria Gray was also better-looking, although a trifle witchlike. She was dressed in black, with a long-sleeved jacket of some sequined material. Her hair was black, turned under slightly — perhaps it was all of this that gave Melrose his impression. Perhaps his mind was tired, what with the drive itself, the trumped-up mechanical trouble, and Dartmoor. As they had walked up to the house earlier, even though scarcely noon, their feet were buried in mist, which rose until the trees were gloved in fog.

"I like your dress, Victoria," said Jessica, who was herself quite dressed up in a blue frock.

Victoria Gray looked at Jessica with a frown. (It seemed compliments from Jessica were rare enough to be suspect.) "You do? Thank you."

"It's beautiful. All spangly. It makes you look ever so much younger."

Robert Ashcroft looked at his niece sharply and then laughed it off. His instinct was probably right. Calling attention to Jessica's rudeness might only have made the matter worse, though Victoria seemed to take it in stride.

"That's why I wore it," she said. "Takes at least a hundred years off my age. What about you, Jessica? It's the first time I've seen you out of your mechanic's outfit in ages. And what have you done to Henry? It looks like a ribbon in his collar."

Since it was difficult to see Henry's collar, buried as it was in his furled skin, the bow peeked out as a tiny ruff of green.

"I dressed him up for company. It matches his eyes."

Ashcroft was surprised. "Henry's eyes? Didn't know he had any."

"You *know* he has green eyes," Jess said, looking innocently into their guest's own.

However unprepared Mulchop was to be butler, Mrs. Mulchop certainly wasn't to be cook. Smoked salmon, double consommé and roast duckling with a mararet stuffing unlike anything Melrose had tasted before. He would like to have the recipe to give to his own cook, he said.

It was Sara Millar who told him: "Herbs and such, and mushrooms, anchovies and poached sweetbreads. Delicious, isn't it?"

Jessie, who had just taken a bite of this delicacy, stared at her plate. "Yuck! Why didn't somebody *tell* me?" She pushed the offending stuffing onto her small bread and butter dish and set it on the floor. "There, Henry," she said sweetly.

"No feeding Henry *at the table*, Jess," said Ashcroft.

Melrose had until then been unaware that Henry made one of their party. It also surprised him that, rather than Jessica's insisting she sit next to the fascinating stranger, she had allowed Sara that honor.

"You must forgive Jessie," said Victoria.

No one looked in less need of forgiveness.

"Poor Henry." Jessie sighed, as if the world were against him, and reached down to pat him in a lightning gesture that rid her plate of a particularly uninteresting turnip that had been lolling there. Then she set about eagerly eating her potatoes and making conversation before someone noticed the gap. "Lord Ardry . . ."

"Lady Jessica?"

"Oh, don't call me *that!*"

"All right, if you don't call me 'lord.' The family name is Plant. It's really horribly complicated, isn't it?"

"Yes. My father's name was Ashcroft. But he was also the Earl of Clerlew."

Ashcroft said, "You mean Curlew. Eat your dinner, Jess." Robert Ashcroft seemed disturbed by all of this talk of lineage.

"I can't eat, not after you told me about the *brains*." She readdressed herself to Melrose. "My mother's name was Barbara Allan." Pointing her fork at the wall opposite, she said, "That's her portrait. Wasn't she beautiful?"

The picture hung behind Robert Ashcroft, who, Melrose saw, had put down his fork. He also seemed to have lost his appetite.

The Countess of Ashcroft was indeed beautiful — slender, tall, dark and wearing a smile that implied having one's picture painted was silly.

"She was also very nice," said Victoria Gray. "So was James, her husband."

Undercurrents, thought Melrose. Or an actual undertow.

Jessica, however, was not going to let her mother's reputation hang by this slender thread of "goodness." "She had a very tragic life —"

Her uncle said, "Leave it alone, Jessie. *Mulchop* — stop lolling there and bring us some more wine!"

Melrose suspected that Ashcroft merely wanted to get their attention away from the Countess of Ashcroft.

It was no deterrent to Jessica. "Grandmother Ashcroft was mad because my mother was only a commoner and her family was in trade. My father always thought that was a good joke. 'In trade.' You can make a lot of money 'in trade,' he kept saying. Like being shopkeepers, if you have a lot of shops."

Robert interrupted. "I don't think our guest is interested in the family tree, Jess."

But Jessica continued to wash the dirty linen. "There was one of them that ran a pub. . . ." As she continued the Barbara Allan saga, it was clear that not only did the Allans have the money, but that hearts had shattered to smithereens wherever the woman walked.

Victoria told her to stop exaggerating and stubbed out her cigarette violently.

"I'm *not!* It's just like the song — isn't it, Uncle Rob. You told me."

Ashcroft smiled and clipped the end of a cigar. "I'm not sure who told who at this point. There seem to be a few frills and furbelows that I don't remember."

In her gossipy way, Jessica went on: "She was lots younger than my father. . . . Though there's nothing wrong with that. I think it's all awfully romantic. But Gran thought it was just to get the title and was furious about it —"

Sara Millar broke in: "I don't think all of this should be trotted out in front of well, *two* relative strangers, Jessica." Her voice was soft and pleasant.

Melrose wanted to laugh. In Jessica Ashcroft he had an unexpected ally. She would make sure he stayed and *stayed,* as long as he took Miss Millar when he left. Romantic things like that happened in Jessica's mind, he was sure. In this case, the romance would also be most fortuitous.

The subject of the recent murders came up — was brought up by Jessica, that is — when they were seated in the drawing room with coffee and cigars and cigarettes.

Robert Ashcroft and Sara Millar were seated side by side on the small sofa. Melrose regarded it as a marvel of logistics, the way Jessica worked herself round to sit between them. She was merely leaning against the arm of the sofa when she said, "The vicar's son. It was really grisly —"

While Jessica enjoyed the grisliness, Melrose studied the portrait of James Ashcroft, which hung above the marble fireplace. He only half-heard the conversation while he thought about James Ashcroft. Clerihew. Curlew. An easy enough error to make . . .

When Melrose turned his attention back to the conversation, he heard Jessica talking about the boy in Dorchester —

Magically, she was now sitting between the two grown-ups.

"Bed, Jessie," said Ashcroft.

"Very well." She sighed. "I only wish I could go for a ride tomorrow."

"That," said Victoria, "is one of the few positive things I think I've heard from you. It's about time I put you up on that horse —"

"*Horse?* Who said *horse?* I mean a motorcar. Sara and Mr. Plant haven't had any rides at all in your cars. Couldn't Mr. Plant drive your Aston?" She looked at Melrose. "It goes from zero to sixty in five-point-two seconds."

"It might, but I doubt *I* could go from zero to one in under an hour. Must be the Dartmoor air." He yawned.

"*You* want to ride around Dartmoor, Jess?" Ashcroft said. "You're always telling me how boring it is."

"That's only because we *live* here. It's always boring where you live. But they'd like it —" She looked from Sara to Melrose. "Just as long as we stay away from Wistman's Wood and the Hairy Hands. *Come on,* Henry."

And she and the dog walked slowly off to bed.

II

Victoria Gray was arranging flowers in a shallow cut-glass bowl for the circular table when Melrose came down for breakfast. She was dressed in riding togs.

"Good morning, Lord Ardry." She cut the stem of one last chrysanthemum, stuck it in the center of her arrangement, and stepped back to look at it with a critical eye much like a painter evaluating his canvas. "Will it do?"

Melrose smiled. "Very nicely, I'd say. Am I the last one down?"

"Except for Jessie. She said she had a sick-headache, and asked to be excused from your excursion into the wilds of Dartmoor."

"I see. But she was to be our tour-guide."

Victoria smiled. "She told me to give you this map. As far as I can see, it's to be a grim tour. Wynchcoombe, Clerihew Marsh, Princetown. I'll have coffee with you, if you don't mind. All the food's still warm, though Mulchop did his best to wrestle it off the sideboard."

"Mind? Indeed not. One gets tired of breakfasting by oneself." Just as one, thought Melrose, gets tired of talking like a peer of the realm. Melrose was having difficulty with his earldom, a difficulty he had never had before he gave up his title. He was perfectly happy talking like a commoner *then*. He felt like someone Jury had dragged out of a ditch, dusted off, and said, "Okay. You'll do."

On the sideboard was a lavish display, all kept cozily warm in their silver dishes. He spooned up some kidney, took a portion of buttered eggs, layered on a couple of rashers of bacon, and helped himself to toast and butter. Then he frowned at his plate and wondered if a peer would gorge himself in this fashion.

Victoria Gray helped herself to toast and coffee. When she had settled at the table across from him, Melrose said, "If you don't mind my saying it — you don't fit the stereotype of 'housekeeper.' "

She laughed. "If you mean changing the linen and towels and wearing keys at my waist — no, I don't. This position is a sinecure. I do take care of the horses pretty much — Billy's a bit lazy — type the odd letter or two for Robert, and arrange flowers." She smiled. "Barbara — Lady Ashcroft — and I were first cousins, though she was born in Waterford. County Waterford. A typical Irish colleen, she was. We were also very good friends. Barbara made an excellent marriage — well, she deserved it, didn't she . . . ?"

She seemed to be talking to herself. Or in the manner of one who is addressing an intimate acquaintance.

"The late Lady Ashcroft was Irish? You mean her daughter's tale of gloom and doom is true?"

"Of course not. Barbara didn't leave a trail of fallen hearts behind her like petals in the dust." She paused. "At least not knowingly."

He wondered what she meant by that. Barbara Ashcroft's face looked down at him from the far wall. The smile was inscrutable, a Mona Lisa smile. "If that portrait doesn't flatter her —"

"Flatter —?" Victoria Gray turned to look. "Oh, not at all. If anything it diminishes her beauty. Jessica will be that beautiful too, one day. You can see it when she isn't dressed in that oily overall she loves to wear and carrying tools around."

"She's quite the mechanic."

"Jessie? She doesn't know a battery from a silencer. I'll bet she told you it was your carburetor."

"Right."

"Her favorite word."

Melrose laughed. "Well, she needs some sort of occupational therapy, wouldn't you say?"

"Believe me, she's got an occupation — though I don't know how therapeutic it is. Keeping her beloved uncle from marrying." She picked up a piece of toast and munched it; then she said, "It's fortunate for Jess that Dartmoor isn't peopled with eligible women."

Seeing the faraway look on her face, Melrose wondered if the fortune weren't divided.

"Why do you think she's been through such a string of governesses?"

"Didn't know she had been." He accepted another cup of coffee from Victoria's hand. "Tell me: why did the Ashcrofts not make the obvious choice and have *you* take care of Jessica? You say your job is a sinecure: seems to me it'd simplify things all around."

Victoria laughed. "Precisely because I *would* take care of her. Did you ever see a child so indulged? I wondered when Robert would get wise and choose a tutor himself, like Sara Millar."

But she did not look at all as if she felt the choice had been wise. She looked, indeed, inexpressibly sad. Melrose could read it in her face: if only Robert Ashcroft's feelings were as certain as this sinecure of a post she held.

III

He had asked Victoria if there was some writing-paper about, and was now sitting in the drawing room, looking up again at the portrait of the rather formidable Earl of Curlew. He then wrote no more than a couple of sentences on the rich, cream-laid Ashcroft stationery, took another sheet and wrote the same sentences. Then, he addressed both to Jury — one to his flat in Islington; the other to him at the Devon-Cornwall headquarters. If he posted them today, Jury would be bound to get one tomorrow, whether in London or Devon.

Melrose stood beneath the portrait, holding out a finger length-wise, and squinted, in this way ridding James Ashcroft of his full mustache. There was a strong resemblance between the brothers. As Curlew resembled Clerihew.

TWENTY

T least, thank God, it was a closed car. The mist
looked as if it meant to hang about all morning,
making distances deceptive, bringing the giant tors closer
than they actually were. The moorland ponies were huddled
against the leeward wall with that instinct they had for an
approaching storm.

And, thank God, she was not one to feel sorry for herself. It
was only owing to Melrose's judicious questioning that Sara
was telling him the story of her life, a life she had herself described as placid, at best; at worst, dull. To Melrose, however, it sounded like neither — more a Dickensian tale of
abandonment and woe. There was the boardinghouse
through whose portal she had been shepherded by the aunt
into whose care she had been given when Sara's mother died.
It was run by an iniquitous woman, Mrs. Strange, the embod-
iment of her name, said Sara.

"Fiery red hair she had that looked like a tent right after
she'd washed it. I suppose, though, I ought to be grateful to
her. Since she was lazy and I was older than the others, and
hadn't much to say in the matter, the care of them often fell

to me. So did my own education. I had to read a lot, as she kept me out of school. To take care of the children."

"Good Lord, why should you feel 'grateful'? You might have gone on to do something more suited to your intelligence than acting as overseer to other people's children."

"Thanks. I had only the one good reference, really. But as it came from a countess, Mr. Ashcroft seemed suitably impressed. I'm fond of children."

"I'm fond of ducks. It doesn't mean I want them running round under my feet all day."

Sara laughed. "With Jessica, it's not being underfoot that I'm in danger of; it's more in being undermined. She doesn't care for me too much."

"On the contrary," said Melrose, slowing to peer through the fog at a signpost, "as we were walking up to the house, she was singing your praises."

"That in itself's suspect, since I'd only just arrived the day before. I wonder how long I'll last? Mr. Ashcroft said his niece was running through tutors at the speed of, well, this car. There were three of us to be interviewed in London. I suppose he winnowed out the rest by mail. Given the salary he offered, he must have been deluged. It's a post anyone would give her eyeteeth for." She paused for a moment, and then went on. "It's rather odd, though . . ."

"Odd, how?"

"To do the interviews that way. It was rather like being cast for a role." She paused. "I only wish I knew the script." She sounded uneasy about her new post.

"Ashcroft strikes me as an amiable, informal chap. Unlikely he's reading from a script."

" 'Amiable'? He certainly is. And goes to no end of trouble for Jessica. I only meant I wonder why he held those interviews in London rather than at Ashcroft?"

"Perhaps because the Lady Jessica wasn't having too much luck herself in choosing the proper person." He slowed the car again to look at another signpost, trying to bury his question — "When was this unnerving interview? Sounds a bit Jamesian to me. Think I'll turn here" — in a comment about their direction.

"What do you mean by Jamesian?"

"*The Turn of the Screw*. The governess goes up to London and finds a handsome, prospective —" Melrose didn't go on. Probably, he was embarrassing her.

"When was the interview? Just a few days ago. The thirteenth. Why?"

"No reason. Will this mist never rise?"

As Melrose negotiated a sharp turn on the narrow road, she said, "Isn't this signposted for Wynchcoombe? And isn't that where the little boy was murdered?"

"Don't you want to go there?"

"Frankly, no." She shivered.

"Oh, come on. Be a sport. Can't we be just a couple of bloodthirsty thrill-seekers?"

Sara laughed. "Do you hang around accident sites?"

"Of course."

II

The vestry of Wynchcoombe Church was still sealed off. A constable stood on the walk outside as stiffly relentless as a horseguard at Buckingham Palace. The rest of the church, though, was open to worshippers and visitors.

"I don't know that I want to go in," said Sara, "now we're here."

"Superstitious?"

"No, afraid," she said quite simply.

Melrose would have made a burnt offering of his Silver Ghost to have a look in the choir vestry, but the presence of another policeman told him there'd be no joy there. The constable, however, seemed to be finding a bit of joy from a *Playboy* magazine, turning it sideways and upside down to get the full effect of a centerfold who must have managed an extremely acrobatic position for the photographer.

Nothing ventured, nothing gained, thought Melrose. At least this policeman looked a bit more human, lacking in granite calm of the constable outside.

Thus, while Sara walked down the nave, Melrose moved to the vestry door, taking out his visiting-card case. He handed the P.C. his card. "Don't suppose there's a chance of getting in there . . . ?"

"About as much as getting into Buckingham Palace," said the P.C., pleased he had precedence over a peer.

Melrose went to join Sara Millar. She was studying a small picture of the sacrifice of Isaac.

"The God of the Old Testament didn't pull his punches, did he?" said Melrose. "Job, Abraham, voices from whirlwinds." He saw her fingering the silver cross she seemed always to wear. Filtered light from the stained-glass windows made a colored tracery over her pale rose jumper and paler skin. She looked delicate, almost otherwordly, and innocent, as if her youth were still unspent. So engrossed was she with the painting, he thought she hadn't heard him. But she answered, "It's beyond belief. I mean, outside conventional belief. It doesn't count for anything, I think."

Melrose was somewhat astonished at this interpretation of a father's being asked to murder his innocent son. " 'Doesn't count' . . . ? I'm sure Isaac would have felt you to be cold comfort." His smile, when she turned on him, was a little fixed.

She had looked angry; now she looked sad. A woman much like the Dartmoor weather, he thought. Forever changing. Interesting, though.

"I only meant," she said, "that the whole notion of God and Abraham must transcend human understanding."

As they walked over to the other wall, Melrose said, "Then what's the point? What's the point of a moral lesson that requires transcendent vision?" She was reading an account in a glassed-over case about the Devil honoring the church with a visit. "It seems someone who owed him his soul fell asleep in church and Satan simply took the roof off and collected him." Sara shook her head. Melrose was wondering if the vicar would ever appear, or whether this was simply not his day. He looked at his watch. Eleven. The pubs would be open. He was afraid if he didn't divert this discussion, she'd have them stopping here all day talking transcendentalism. "The only way I can justify God's way to man is by malt, as Houseman said."

She smiled slightly. "I take it you noticed the George."

Sara was, in spite of her transcendent streak, quick enough and a good sport. He looked around as the heavy door to the church opened and shut behind an elderly man, who then made his way down the aisle with a proprietary air. Melrose wondered if this might be the Reverend White. Certainly, the man paid no attention at all to the Devon-Cornwall constabulary, so Melrose assumed he was not just another pilgrim. This was borne out by the Devon-Cornwall constabulary's quickly closing his magazine and shoving it under the cushion of his chair.

Melrose told Sara he'd be back in a moment and walked down the aisle in the wake of this white-haired man, making up his excuse as he went.

"Terribly sorry to intrude upon your grief." This comfortless cliché embarrassed Melrose. "You *are* Mr. White?"

The vicar said he was, and appeared to be less griefstricken than a grandfather might have been. Less than Abraham, certainly, and Abraham was only following orders. The vicar's eyes were stony-cold.

"What was it you wanted?"

Melrose removed a card from the gold case that had been his mother's (before Agatha had appropriated it); the cards had been his father's, the seventh Earl of Caverness, and Melrose, the eighth, simply thought what was one earl, more or less?

The vicar read it and handed it back. There was something about one's own card being given back to one that was extremely discouraging.

"Sorry, but should I know you? You're not local. I'm not aware of the family."

Melrose almost wished Agatha had been there to hear *that* judgment passed. He felt a lack of locality stamped on his face, much like the coat-of-arms stamped on the card. "No. My home is in Northamptonshire. The account of your grandson's death in the paper gave the mother's name as Mary O'Brian." Melrose looked up at the intricately painted ceiling-bosses, each one of them apparently different, and wondered what sum of money would entice the vicar to look at life in a more worldly fashion. "You see, years ago we had a Mary O'Brian employed at our home — Ardry End — as upstairs maid."

"Yes? But it's a common name."

Melrose realized he had stirred something in the vicar's breast, for the man's face colored somewhat and he added, "But, then, Mary was a common woman."

Even Melrose, no stickler for men of the cloth being more than human, was a little surprised by this. Apparently the Reverend Mr. White was not worried about the roof caving in. "It's been some years since she was there. I've had a bit of a time tracking her down —"

"That doesn't surprise me — given Mary."

Melrose would have been happy to wander through the dark wood of the vicar's feelings about his daughter-in-law had the vicar shown any sign of wanting to lead him. But the remark simply fell and lay there like a tree across their path.

Mr. White reminded Melrose of someone he couldn't quite place.

"This has to do with a small bequest in my father's will."

"Oh?"

"My father found her to be an especially dependable servant; she went to a great deal of trouble nursing my mother through a long illness —"

"Mary? It's the last thing I'd have expected. At any rate, Mary's dead. Didn't the account mention that?"

Melrose, having seen no obituary, could only say: "Yes, it did." He thought perhaps he shouldn't elaborate on what the "account" *did* tell the world.

"Both of them died in a motorcycle accident. Mary liked fast living. David was in divinity school before he met her. He would perhaps have followed in my footsteps. Then he met Mary." The vicar closed his eyes as if he were hearing the painful news for the first time. "Whatever gift your father wished to bestow upon her . . ." He shrugged.

They had been standing all this time in the aisle. Melrose wished they could sit down, but a church pew seemed an unlikely place for such a conversation.

"Perhaps then you would accept it for the church? In memory of your grandson?"

"David?" One would think he had to be reacquainted with the name.

"I realize five hundred pounds is not all that much —"

The Reverend White looked Melrose up and down. Melrose felt conscious of the suit from his bespoke tailor, the handmade shoes, the silk shirt, the handsome overcoat.

"Well, Lord Ardry, if you consider five hundred pounds meager, you must be wealthy indeed." He managed to make inherited wealth sound like plunder.

"I am," said Melrose simply. "I'll see the bequest is sent to the church, if that's suitable."

"Thank you."

With what struck Melrose as a rather summary dismissal in the circumstances, Mr. White started to turn and leave. "Just one more thing, Mr. White. I was wondering about the Ashcroft family."

With five hundred pounds in the balance, the vicar must have felt something was due this Nosey Parker of an earl. "Wondering what?"

"Well, I've rather made a hobby of heraldry and that sort of thing. How long have the Ashcrofts been feudal overlords of Wynchcoombe and Clerihew Marsh?" The question, of course, would annoy the vicar.

"Feudalism is dead, Lord Ardry. At least the last I heard —"

Melrose smiled fatuously. "Dying, perhaps. But I sometimes wonder if the liberties the feudal barons took were not still being taken . . . ?"

"Sir, I have a very busy schedule."

He seemed willing to look a five-hundred-pound gift-horse in the mouth after all. "I'm sorry. It's just that the Ashcroft family appears to be much the most important family about. James Ashcroft was the Earl of Curlew, wasn't he?"

The vicar frowned. "Yes."

"I just wondered if perhaps 'Curlew' weren't some deviant spelling of 'Clerihew.' Or it would have been the other way round, I mean? 'Clerihew Marsh' ought really to be 'Curlew Marsh.' The curlew being a bird and the crest on the Ashcroft coat-of-arms."

"That is correct." Again he turned to go.

"And your first name, vicar. 'Linley.' James Ashcroft was the Viscount Linley and one of his other names was 'Whyte.' Spelled differently, of course."

"If you're wondering whether I'm a relation of the Ashcrofts, yes, I am. But certainly a very distant one. His bequest to the church was even more surprising than yours. But he was generous, I'll say that for him."

Melrose wondered what the vicar *wouldn't* say for James Ashcroft.

The vicar continued: "I was certainly surprised at his leaving fifty thousand pounds."

So was Melrose.

Sara had been patiently hovering in the shadows all of this time, reading the account of the storm that described a visit from the Devil knocking the spire off the church.

"Sorry," said Melrose.

"Oh, that's all right. Was that the vicar?"

"Yes. I'm thirsty. How about you?"

"I could do with a cup of tea. But I expect you prefer the pub?"

She was certainly agreeable. And attractive. And — well, quite the sort of young woman that a de Winter or a Rochester *might* marry.

No wonder Lady Jessica was trying to hand her over to Melrose.

After they left the church, they stood looking for some moments at the moss- and lichen-veiled headstones.

"Now I remember who the Reverend Mr. White reminds me of. Hester's Chillingworth."

Sara was puzzled. "Chillingworth?"

"You know. *The Scarlet Letter.* I wonder if he looked upon Davey as a benighted little Pearl."

"Whatever were you talking about all that time? You hadn't heard of him before, had you?"

Melrose paused to consider the question and decided two lies were no worse than one. "No. You don't see a post office about, do you? I need to post these letters."

They walked off in search of one. Melrose took the quiet walk as an opportunity to reflect.

TWENTY-ONE

THE cat Cyril sat on Fiona Clingmore's typewriter watching the noonday ritual of the rejuvenation of Fiona's face. Powder, mascara, lip rouge, eyeliner. When Jury walked in, Cyril appeared to have entered into some symbiotic relation with Fiona, in his stately posture on the typewriter, drawing his paw across his face, the student testing the lesson of the master.

There had been a great deal of speculation about the cat's appearance in the halls of New Scotland Yard. It was generally thought that Cyril had discovered the tunnel originally meant for theatergoers to a theater that never materialized and where the headquarters of the Metropolitan Police now sat, owing to some misadventure over cash flow or architectural fault or need. In any event, the cat Cyril had been seen prowling the halls as if his antennae were searching out (like some medium's familiar) the office of Chief Superintendent Racer. With Racer, Cyril enjoyed a slightly different symbiotic relation from the one with Fiona; and in Racer's case, it was doubtful that the relation was of benefit to both. But it certainly seemed to go down a treat with Cyril, who could outwit and outmaneuver Chief Superintendent Racer any day.

It was testimony to Cyril's staying power that he had been hanging around Racer's office for upwards of a year (maybe even two), which was more than could be said of any member of the Met — uniformed, CID, or civilian. Except for Superintendent Jury, whose staying power (and, Jury suspected, slight masochistic streak) matched Cyril's. Fiona, of course, was made of such steely stuff she could have walked under falling ladders or falling bombs and still remained upright. Only such a woman could have stood it as Racer's secretary. She was constantly being told to get the mangy rat-catcher *out* from under Racer's eyes and feet or he'd fire her and kill Cyril. Fiona paid far more attention to refurbishing her eye makeup than she did to the exhortations of her boss. Racer himself had often tossed Cyril out in the hall. But Cyril always returned, like Melville's Bartleby, to sit on a convenient sill and stare from a window at the blind brick wall of another part of the Yard.

Thus both Fiona and Cyril were engaged in their prelunch ablutions when Jury walked into Racer's outer office. "Hullo, Fiona. Hullo, Cyril," said Jury.

Fiona returned the greeting while running her little finger around the corners of her mouth; Cyril's tail twitched. He always appeared happy to see Jury, perhaps out of admiration for a soul-brother, one who could stick it.

"You're early, for once," said Fiona, snapping her mirrored compact shut with a little click. Jury often wondered where she came by these pre–Second World War memorabilia: he hadn't seen a woman with one of those Art Deco compacts since he was a kid. Fiona herself was like an artifact: she had been and still was, in her way, pretty. Pretty like the old photos of movie starlets with cupid-bow mouths and upswept blond hairdos used to be. Jury suspected that Fiona's own yellow curls came from the bottle, neat. That there were some silver threads amongst the gold Fiona had attributed to a good job of frosting at her salon. "He's still at his club," she added.

Jury yawned and scrunched down in his chair. "White's? Boodles? The Turf?"

Fiona laughed and rested her newly primed face on her overlapped hands. "You think one of them would let him in?" She checked a gold circlet of a watch — also from prehistoric digs — and said, "Been gone two hours, so he ought to be popping in any minute."

"Thanks, I'll wait in his office — give him a fright, maybe." He winked at Fiona, who then asked him if he'd eaten yet. It was as much a ritual when Jury was there as the revamping of her face. Jury made his excuses. A policeman's life is full of grief, he told her. It was Racer's cautionary phrase that covered everything from being first on the rota to finding a mass-murderer in your closet.

He noticed as he stood up she was taking out her bottle of nail varnish — a Dracula-like deep purple, almost black. Fiona favored black. All of her outfits — sheer summer frocks, winter wools — were black. Maybe she wanted to be sure she was ready for Racer's funeral.

The cat Cyril, seeing his chance, followed Jury into Racer's *sanctum sanctorum* and plumped himself in the chief's swivel chair. Jury sat in the chair directly across from Cyril and the broad expanse of Racer's empty desk. If there was one thing the chief superintendent believed in, it was delegating authority. Seldom did Jury see folders, notepads, papers — the usual junk — defiling his chief's desk. Jury looked at Cyril, whose head alone could be seen over the top of the desk, and said, "What was it, sir, you wished to see me about? Oh? Yes . . . well, sorry. A policeman's life —"

He hadn't got the end of the old Racer shibboleth out before his chief's spongy step came up behind him. "Talking to yourself again, Jury?" Racer hung his Savile Row overcoat on a coatrack and walked around to his swivel chair. Cyril had slipped like syrup from Racer's chair and was now under the desk to study (Jury was sure) the best avenue of attack.

Racer went on: "Well, it certainly can't be from over*work*, lad. Obviously, you haven't been doing much on the Dorchester case or you'd have *reported in*, now wouldn't you? Not to say anything of the two others murdered! I do not like the Commissioner breathing down my neck, Jury. So what have you got to report. Meaning: what progress have you made?"

Jury told him as much as he felt was necessary for Racer to get the Commissioner off his back. It was, as always, too little for Racer. He would only have been satisfied with Jury's actually producing the murderer right there, in his office.

"That's *all*, Jury?"

"Afraid so."

"As far as I'm concerned — what the hell's *that*?" Racer was looking under his desk. He punched the intercom and demanded Fiona's presence to get the beast out from under his desk. "This ball of mange has used up eight of its nine lives, Miss Clingmore! Swear to God," he muttered, leveling a glance at Jury that suggested Jury might have used up nine-out-of-nine.

Fiona swayed into the office and collected Cyril. Fiona was certainly in no danger of using up *her* lives. The black-patent-leather belt she wore to nip in her waist sent the flesh undulating up and undulating down. Racer's eyes always seemed undecided on which direction to take.

"So go on," said Racer, when Fiona had left.

"Nothing much to be going on with. Sir." Jury always hesitated a little before the *sir*.

And Racer always noticed it. Thus Jury was in for the "ever-since-you-made-superintendent" lecture, one that Racer must have practiced in his sleep, so refined had it become, so ornamental — like intaglio figurines around a priceless vase. There was always something new to comment on, regarding the skill of the artisan.

Jury yawned.

"Where the hell's Wiggins? What's he been up to, except contaminating the Dorset police?"

Jury made no comment other than to say Sergeant Wiggins was in Devon.

"You do realize, don't you, how this psycho has hit the press? Three kids dead, Jury, *three*." He held up his fingers in case Jury didn't understand the word itself. "And you can't nail one of these suspects?"

"Not on the evidence we have now, no. I want to see the Ashcroft solicitor."

"Then get the hell out and go and see him. I've got enough work to do as it is." The pristine condition of his desk did not attest to this.

II

"Robert Ashcroft? But I've known him as long as I've known — knew — his brother James." He got up from his chair to pace several yards of cushioned carpet.

Mr. Mack, Jury decided, was solicitor to more than one moneyed family, given his surroundings: thick carpet, good prints on the walls, mahogany furniture, including the desk that shimmered like a small dark lake beneath its coats of beeswax. Its principal ornament was an elegant bronze cat, probably some pricey Egyptian artifact.

What interested Jury was that Mack did not simply reject the idea of imposture out of hand. Perhaps he was simply a very cautious fellow who would see all of the facets of an argument, no matter how prismatic.

His pacing was interrupted by the entrance of his secretary bearing a number of documents. His glance strayed up to Jury occasionally, as if he were turning the idea over as he turned the pages before him, signing each with a flourish.

The young lady who was Mack's secretary was the antithesis of Fiona Clingmore. One could tell her dress was expensive, not by its showiness but by the cut of the cloth. She was herself — hair, skin, nails — as polished as the desk itself.

But she lacked that certain something — that nice seamy presence which was the Fiona *brio*. Indeed, Jury wondered, as he watched the solicitor signing papers, if, in his realm of Ideas, Plato wouldn't have plumped for Racer, Fiona and Cyril, instead of Mack, Miss Chivers and the bronze cat.

Mr. Mack recapped his pen and Miss Chivers gathered up the papers and slid softly out, hazarding another look at Jury as she left. He smiled. She blushed.

Mack returned to the question of the Ashcroft identity. "No, it's improbable, Mr. Jury, that this Robert Ashcroft is not the real one. As you say, there was no one in the household who had known him, and the relations were all distant ones — but, no. When the will was probated, we certainly asked for Robert's bona fides — indeed, we did that of everyone. Victoria Gray, for example."

"I wasn't aware she came into a part of the Ashcroft fortune."

"She certainly did. Not much as an outright legacy, but a very substantial legatee were something to happen to Jessica. Very substantial. And insofar as Robert himself is concerned, I'm quite satisfied." He had resumed his seat and rested his chin on the tips of his fingers, prayerfully.

"What about other bequests? Any other substantial ones?"

"Yes. There was one to a church. And also to his wife's former nurse, Elizabeth. She was a cousin of Lady Ashcroft's." He ran a finger over the bronze cat. "Not a very pleasant person, as I recall." A heave of shoulders here. After all, solicitors can't be choosers. "But the thing is, you see, none of these were outright bequests. I didn't care for it, but there it was. All of the money went to Jessica."

"You mean, that as long as Jessica Ashcroft is alive, no one gets anything?"

Mr. Mack shook his head. "James Ashcroft wanted everything to go to Jessie. She can, of course, when she comes of age, honor those bequests immediately. Until that time, Robert is executor of the will and receives a fair allowance —"

"What's 'fair'?"

"I believe in the neighborhood of five thousand pounds a year."

Jury shook his head. "That'd be a slum for Ashcroft. It certainly wouldn't do much by way of supporting his habit. No, no, Mr. Mack —" The solicitor's eyes had widened. "— not drugs. Motorcars. Vintage, classic, antique."

"Ah, yes. Well, Robert has access to Jessica's money, you see. All he need do is apply to me. If I think the expense suitable, I let him have it. You're quite right, those cars of his are pricey. But a drop in the bucket when we're talking millions of pounds. James and Robert were extremely close. Even when Robert went to Australia, they wrote to one another regularly. Those letters, you see, were paramount in establishing authenticity. Why are you suspicious of Robert Ashcroft, anyway?"

"No reason, except for the convenient arrangement of the household. Even the relations who came to the funeral hadn't seen him in a long time, if at all."

"Yes, that's true. When that much money and property's at stake, odd lots of relations come crawling out of the woodwork, some of them hoping to break a will unfair to them. Claiming what they consider their 'fair share,' or claiming the one who gets the lion's share isn't really the lion." Mr. Mack allowed himself a little purse-lipped smile.

"So the brother James more or less allowed Robert *carte blanche*?"

Mack frowned. "Yes. And I frankly don't approve of open-ended arrangements like that. Messy." He squared a cigarette box and adjusted the alignment of the bronze cat. "But James had the devil's own trust in Robert." There was another fussy little smile. "Not the best way of putting it, perhaps. But the other relations, by blood or by marriage, were rather a sorry lot. So far as I could see, they had absolutely no claim on the money, not to say upon James's affections. But he was — I advised him to do so — smart enough to leave small sums to the ones whom he felt would be the troublemakers."

"I'd like to see a copy of that will, Mr. Mack."

Mr. Mack rocked back in his chair. "Is that really necessary?"

Jury smiled. "I'd like to see it, necessary or not. The will's been probated. Public property now."

"Hmm. Very well. Miss Chivers can make you up a copy." He punched his intercom and gave his secretary directions.

"And I'd also like to see those letters."

"The ones from James? Well, Robert has them, of course." Mr. Mack frowned. "Are you suggesting an analysis of the handwriting?"

"Something like that, yes." Jury thought, really, that the Ashcroft solicitors would have done it themselves. He rose to go. "Thanks for your help, Mr. Mack."

On the way out he collected the copy of the Ashcroft will and another appraising glance from Miss Chivers.

Mr. Mack's office was in The City. Jury made his way to the Aldgate tube stop, wondering what was bothering him. Something he'd seen? Something he'd heard? James Ashcroft's will was thick. There was a great deal of property. The will had been signed by Ashcroft, witnessed by Mack and two other solicitors. One of the names was George Thorne.

George Thorne. Again.

Jury changed at Baker Street to get the Northern line and, as he waited for his train, looked over the tiled wall of the platform, where the profile of Sherlock Holmes had been wonderfully contrived during the station's renovation. It was a hard act to follow.

III

"So sad it is," said Mrs. Wasserman, who lived alone in the basement flat of the building in Islington. Jury's own flat was on the second floor, but he had stopped off to see how she was doing. To admit him, she had had to throw two bolts, release a chain, and turn the deadlock. There were grilles over her windows, too. Mrs. Wasserman could have slept with ease in the middle of the Brixton riots. But Mrs. Wasserman was never at ease, except when the superintendent was around who mercifully (for her) lived upstairs.

They were eating her homemade strudel and drinking coffee and she was talking about the case Jury was on. "I know you don't discuss," she said, "but it frightens me to death to see these children—" Unable to bring it out, she stopped, shook her head, drank her coffee. "I know you don't say, of course you can't, but this person, he must be crazy." And she made a tiny circle round her ear to demonstrate craziness.

"I expect so, Mrs. Wasserman. We don't know the motive."

"Motive? Who says motive? Crazies don't *have* them, Mr. Jury." Her smile was slight and forgiving, as if she couldn't expect this novice policeman to know everything, could she?

Indeed she was right on that count. "Psychotics do have motives, even if the motives are irrational and obscure. Or displaced."

"What is that, *displaced*?" She was suspicious of psychoanalytic jargon.

"Just that the killer's actual object isn't the person he kills."

She thought this over, chewing her strudel. "What a hideous waste of time." Mournfully, she glanced up at him. "The papers, Mr. Jury, are full of it."

Jury knew about the papers. And he also knew he had described, without consciously meaning to, Mrs. Wasserman's own phobia. How old had she been during the Second World War? Fifteen, sixteen perhaps. Whatever horrors she had suffered then had gone underground, submerged in her mind, but bonded to that scrap of memory she could stand — the Stranger who followed her, whose step behind her she could pick out of a hundred footsteps, whose description Jury had taken down in his notebook time and time again, knowing there was no such person. And it was Jury who had helped her with the locks, the chains, the bolts. Mrs. Wasserman could have written the book on agoraphobia.

Jury looked at her windows, grilles and shutters. He looked at her door, locked and bolted. "You bolt the door —" He really hadn't meant to say it aloud.

"Pardon? Of course I bolt the door." Her large breasts shook with laughter. "*You*, of all people! You helped me with the bolts." Then she grew concerned. "It's sleep you need, Mr. Jury. You never get enough. Sometimes it is not until two or three in the morning you get in."

Jury only half-heard her. His eye was still fixed on that impregnable door. "But what, exactly, does it keep out?"

She seemed puzzled, suspicious even — in the way one is suspicious that a dear friend might be going off the rails. "Why, Him, of course. As you know."

And she went back calmly to eating her strudel.

TWENTY-TWO

I T was five miles on the other side of Dorchester, in Win terbourne Abbas, that it hit him — what had seemed in significant at the time. Jury pulled into a petrol station, aske for a phone and was told there was one in the Little Che next door.

The restaurant was almost antiseptically clean, right dow to the starched uniforms of the waitresses. Jury asked for . coffee, said he'd be back in a moment. He put in a call to th Devon-Cornwall headquarters and was told that the divi sional commander was in Wynchcoombe.

It was TDC Coogan in the mobile unit there who told Jur (testily, he thought) that Macalvie had taken Sergeant Wig gins and gone to the Poor Struggler to make "inquiries." Jur smiled. Although Betty Coogan didn't believe it, Macalvi probably was doing just that. She gave him the number.

Jury could hear Elvis Presley in the background singing "Hound Dog" after someone answered the telephone at th Poor Struggler. Not Freddie, probably the regular who hap pened to be nearest the phone.

"Don't know him, mate. Mac-who?"

Jury could almost hear the phone being wrenched from the ther's hand, along with a brief exchange that had Macalvie orking the old Macalvie charm, complete with expletives. Macalvie here." And he turned away to shout to Freddie to urn the damned music down or he'd have her license. "Maalvie," he said again.

"What are you doing there, Macalvie?"

"Oh, it's you." There was the usual lack of enthusiasm for Jew Scotland Yard. "Talking to your friend. The one passing imself off as a bloody earl. Seems okay, though."

Macalvie always seemed to like the very people Jury was ure he'd hate. He cut across the latest Macalvie theory by elling him what he'd learned from Mr. Mack.

"*Thorne?* He was one of the Ashcroft bunch. When? I nean for how long?"

"I don't know. Get one of your men to give him a call. Viggins there?"

"Yeah, sure." Macalvie seemed to be carrying Wiggins round in his pocket. "For God's sakes, I should have known bout Thorne."

"Why? You're not a mind reader."

There was a small pause, as if Macalvie were debating this oint. "Yeah. What do you want to tell Wiggins?"

"Just let me talk to him."

"It's a secret between you two?"

"No. I want to check something. Stop pouting and put him n."

"Sir!" Wiggins was probably standing at attention.

Jury sighed. "As you were, Sergeant. Listen: when we were n the Rileys' flat, or as we were leaving, that is, you noticed a ramed document above the mantel —"

"That's right. Mrs. Riley was a nurse. Had been, I mean."

"What name was on it?" Wiggins was not always spot-on vhen it came to sifting facts down to a solution, but he could

usually be counted on to remember the facts themselves. A
master of minutiae.

There was a silence on the other end of the telephone
Wiggins was thinking; Jury let him. Jury also thought he
heard paper crackle. Opening another packet of Fisherman's
Friends, probably. "Elizabeth Allan, sir."

"That's what I thought, Wiggins. Thanks. And thank Plant
for his letter. I got it this morning." Jury hung up. He paid for
his coffee but didn't bother drinking it.

II

"What's me being a nurse got to do with it?" asked Beth
Riley. "What's it to do with Simon?"

"Maybe nothing, maybe a lot," said Jury, replenishing her
glass with the bottle of Jameson's he'd the foresight to bring
along. The glass in her hand welcomed the bottle in Jury's.
She sat in the same cabbage rose chair she had the first time
Jury had visited their lodgings. The husband wasn't here
today, and she seemed to be trying to make up her mind
whether she was flattered or a little frightened that it was she
whom the superintendent wanted to see. "So given you were
nurse to Lady Ashcroft before she died, and also her cousin,
you knew Jessica and Robert Ashcroft."

Her answer was surly. "Yes. Not all that well. Jessica was
only a baby, and the brother — I'd seen him at the Eaton
Square house in London off and on. That was before Barbara
got so sick she needed someone all the time."

"Is he much changed?"

"Changed? That's an odd question. Though I guess ten
years in Australia's enough to change anyone."

"I mean, did he appear as you remembered him?"

Again, she frowned. "Well, yes — wait a tic." She leaned
toward Jury, the flashy rhinestone brooch winking in the
light of the lamp. "Are you telling me that's not Robert Ash-

croft?" Obviously, no news could have pleased her more. Mrs. Riley had been the most adamant of the relatives who questioned James Ashcroft's will.

"No," said Jury, watching her hope dissipate along with the John Jameson's. He calculated that somewhere during the third drink she'd reach the confessional stage. "No, I'm stumbling in the dark, hoping I'll fall over the right answer." He smiled.

Beth Riley, cushioned by cabbage rose pillows and Jameson's, gave him a once-over that strongly suggested she wouldn't mind being what he fell over. Once again, she held out her glass. Self-pity would take over pretty soon, he knew. He was happy to help it along. He poured her a third drink and looked at the display over the mantel: the nursing degree with its gold seal, the family photographs, the mahogany-backed coat-of-arms. The same coat-of-arms, emblazoned here, that Jury had seen on the writing-paper, the note that Plant had sent him. It was the crest, the curlew embellished as carefully as some monk's Biblical illumination.

"They're none of us perfect," said Beth. "I made a mess of things, marrying as I did. Oh, not that Al's not a good *provider* . . ."

Jury wanted to steer clear of Riley's good points, which were certain to end with the bad. He was interested in facts, not in her soul-searching, the whys and wherefores of her marriage. "What was — or is — your relation to the Ashcroft family, Mrs. Riley?"

"You can call me Beth." Over the rim of her glass she looked at him coyly.

Jury assumed he'd damned well *better* call her Beth if he wanted information. He smiled a warm, insincere smile. "Beth. Your relation with the Ashcrofts?"

"To hear *him* talk — that Robert — I'd no more to do with them than the horses in the stableyard."

(Jury thought that Robert was probably right.)

"I was cousin to Barbara. *First* cousin." She made sure he understood that it was no fly-by-night relationship. "We were both born in County Waterford. I came to England when I was small, long before Barbara." She said it as if this gave her some proprietarial right over the country which Barbara lacked. "But I hardly ever saw them until she got sick. Just trust that kind of people to want your help, and then not to remember how much help you gave."

"But Ashcroft certainly did remember, Beth. You'd come into a sizable sum." He paused. "If anything happened to Jessica Ashcroft."

"What's likely to happen to *her?*" The whiskey hadn't softened her up enough, apparently. Nor did she respond to the implication of what Jury had said. "That's no way to leave an inheritance — you have to wait until somebody *dies*. It's Riley, that's what it is! Robert Ashcroft is too much of a snob to have us round. But then they always were the worst kind of snobs."

Jury was sympathetic as he topped off her glass. "That does seem a bit unfair."

She hooted. "Unfair? *I'll* say it's unfair. Listen: we were perfectly willing to take the girl in, to be mum and dad to her —"

(Like you were mum to Simon, Jury thought.)

"— but, no. She was handed over bag and baggage to him. As if he'd ever done a thing in his life for the child." She turned on Jury one of the most vindictive smiles he'd ever seen. "Though I wouldn't deny he might have done a good deal for the mother. Barbara."

The implication was clear. But Jury didn't want to give her the satisfaction, at the moment, of indulging her fantasies.

They were interrupted by her husband's coming into the sitting room, dazzled to see Jury there, as if he'd stepped into white light from the darkness of a theater. He blinked. "Superintendent?"

Jury rose. "Mr. Riley." They shook hands. "I was just asking your wife a few questions that I thought might be relevant to Simon's death. I've got to be going now."

Riley led him to the top of the stairs. He looked back over his shoulder, then whispered to Jury. "She gets a bit tearful after a drink. Not much of a drinker, is Beth. What about Simon?"

"Nothing new, I'm afraid. I was just trying to sort out the family connections. You see, I didn't know your wife was related to the Ashcroft family."

He was not so far gone in sorrow that he couldn't laugh at this. "You must be the only one in Dorchester who doesn't know it, then. What a row she made after the funeral." He sighed. "Water under the bridge, why quarrel? Are you anywhere nearer finding out who did this?"

Jury debated his answer. "Yes, I think so, Mr. Riley."

"Dear God, I hope so. After reading about the other two — it's a dreadful thing to say, Mr. Jury,"— another confession —"but I'm glad Simon wasn't in it alone." He gave Jury a furtive look, as if there stood the messenger of God who would condemn him to the everlasting fire for such a thought. "I can't help it."

"I know. I only wish I could."

And Jury went down the stairs and out of Riley's: Fine Meat and Game.

TWENTY-THREE

THE black cat, tail twitching, sat on the stone balustrade tracking the progress of two seagulls on their unwary way toward half a discarded sandwich. When Jury's appearance disturbed this tableau — the oafish stranger walking between the tourist's camera and its vision of scenic wonders — the cat turned its yellow eyes on Jury as if any sacrificial victim were better than none. Then it jumped down and walked over to sit on the stone step and stare the door out of countenance. There was food in there somewhere.

Jury was surprised to see the curtains undrawn. And she must have been watching from a window, because the door opened as he raised his hand to knock. The cat marched straight in.

Molly looked down and up and smiled. "He'll make straight for the kitchen and glare until I give him something. Come on in."

He felt an odd reluctance to put his foot over the sill. The sensation might have been something akin to what a medium feels when suddenly, across a sill, there's a cold spot. It only lasted a second or two, his hesitation, but she noticed it. Her smile now seemed almost left over, and she glanced at the windows as if she'd like to close the curtains, in the way she had just, in a flash, drawn one across her smile.

He had let her down, the last thing he wanted to do. But with Molly Singer he supposed it would be very difficult not to; it was not that she expected too much of the world, but that she expected too little.

She took his coat and went to feed the cat. From the kitchen she asked him if he'd like some coffee and, in an attempt at banter, told him he'd better take her up on the offer; it didn't come round often. He could not see her, only hear her. Her voice was strained as it hadn't been when he'd come to the door.

"Then you'd better bring it quick," he called back.

She must have had it ready, for she brought it in straightaway, after he'd heard dry food rattle into a bowl.

They went through the business of how much sugar and cream, and she had some toasted teacakes, which she cut with a knife that might have done them more service in cutting the tension. Finally, she said, "It was nice of you to send the message you were coming." She was studying her teacake. "I don't think Superintendent Macalvie would have."

Certainly, *that* couldn't have been truer. "You know police." He nodded toward the kitchen door where the black cat was washing its kingly self. "We're worse than *him*. Hell on wheels, beat down doors, storm right in." Jury mustered the best smile he could.

It was, apparently, good enough, for the invisible curtain opened and she said, "You didn't. You're not very frightening for a policeman, Mr. Jury."

"Richard. For God's sakes, don't tell Macalvie I don't scare people. He'll send me back to London."

"I doubt one just sends Scotland Yard 'back to London.'"

Jury laughed, and she sat back with her coffee and relaxed a little. Today, she had relinquished her Oxfam-special for what looked more like Jaeger — a wool dress in such a warm shade of gold she should have been able to cut through the cold spot, send the ghosts packing, tame the demons. She couldn't. Could anyone? "Macalvie —" He hadn't meant to say it aloud. He added quickly, laughing again. "You don't know Macalvie. . . ."

Although he hadn't meant to bring it up that way, or to make light of her dilemma, he knew it was as good a way as any. So he didn't retract when he saw the look on her face, a look of disappointment replaced quickly with a getting-down-to-business smile. He thought of that scene in the hotel. Molly could rise to an occasion. With a vengeance. That worried him.

"I didn't imagine," she said, "you'd come on a social call."

But one could always hope. Jury said nothing.

"Superintendent Macalvie will twist things into whatever shape suits his purposes."

"No. Macalvie's too good a cop; he doesn't twist things."

As the black cat positioned itself on the twin of Jury's chair and gave him a fiery-gold look, so did Molly Singer. "Well, he might not 'twist' them into shape, but he doesn't seem to mind battering them." She reached down to the bottom shelf of the table by the little couch and brought out a bottle of whiskey. She raised it slightly. "Want some in your coffee?"

Jury shook his head, watching her as she held the bottle on her knee. It was a fresh bottle, and she broke the seal. But she didn't uncap it; she stared at it as if the bottle were an old friend turned stranger. He did not think she really wanted a drink; he thought she wanted something to do for distraction. Her need for something no one was able to give her was so intense, it drained him to think that any comfort he could offer would be pretty cold comfort coming from a policeman.

That's a swell rationalization, Jury, he said to himself. He could have given it. The truth was, there was something about Molly Singer that made him feel afraid of being drawn in.

"Why is Chief Superintendent Macalvie so certain I'm this Mary Mulvanney?"

"She was hard to forget." He smiled. "So would you be."

"Because we throw things?"

"No. You're afraid that Mary Mulvanney would be even more of a suspect?"

"She would be."

"Why?"

"Because Chief Superintendent Macalvie thinks so."

Jury smiled. "He could be wrong."

"Oh? Why don't you try telling him that? Because you value your life." She made a poor attempt at a smile, and then said, not looking at him, "Do you remember what it's like to be in love when you're sixteen?"

"Same thing as when you're forty, I guess." He looked at her long enough to force her to turn her eyes back to his. "Why?"

She sat forward on the couch, slowly, as if she were very tired and, even, very old. "Oh, Superintendent . . ."

You understand nothing. She didn't say it, but from her expression, she might as well have.

Mary Mulvanney would certainly have a reason to hate the world. Indeed, Mary Mulvanney might have become obsessive. Like Molly Singer . . .

"You're thinking the same thing he is."

Jury looked up, surprised. She had been studying his face — carefully, he was sure — for hints of increased suspicions, and found them.

He tried to pass it off with a smile. "You read minds."

Leaning her head against her hand, she returned the smile. And her face had a tinge of the glow it had when he'd first come. "Faces."

That she thought Jury had a particularly nice one was pretty clear, and he looked away, toward the cricket stool where he imagined the house-ghost stirring the ashes. At least her reply brought him to the point: "You'd be pretty good at that, being a photographer." He looked back at her. "We'd like you to do us a favor."

Her head came up from her hand, and her body tensed. Even before he'd asked, she saw the red light of danger. "Me? I can't imagine what."

"There's a place in Dartmoor more or less equidistant from Princetown, Wynchcoombe and Clerihew Marsh." Her expression didn't change. "It's called Ashcroft. Quite a large manor house —"

"Go on." It was as if the suspense that clung to that word *favor* — which could only mean action of some sort — was pulling her from the couch. She was leaning forward, hands clasped so tightly the knuckles were white.

Jury simply brought it out. "We need a photographer —"

"No." She shook her head slowly, her eyes shut. "No."

"Say No, if you want, but let me finish. There's a little girl in that house; she's ten years old. She's the sole heir to the Ashcroft millions. Her father was a peer. There've already been three children murdered, Molly. We're not looking forward to a fourth."

Molly looked up then, astonishment stamped on her face. "Whatever it is you want from *me* — dear God, *why?* I'm your main *suspect!*"

"A suspect. Okay, I won't deny it, though I doubt you had anything to do with these killings." Doubt was not certainty; but the doubt was strong.

Astonishment gave way to something like hope and a half-smile. "You're outvoted."

"Macalvie?" Jury smiled. "Then it's one against one. Not outvoted."

"If Chief Superintendent Macalvie has the other vote, believe me, you're outvoted. But go on. I'll just say no at the end, but go on."

"We want pictures — photographs — of, well, everything.

Your bona fides are all arranged. There's an expensive, sleek new magazine that specializes in classic and antique cars. You're their top photographer: and you know what a professional does because you've done it." He smiled. "Piece of cake."

"Dipped in cyanide. Are you crazy?" Her voice was going up a ladder of tension. "Richard—"

As she leaned toward him, he felt his name in her mouth as something strange, saltwater on the tongue. "Molly." Again he smiled.

Quickly she looked away, and for something to do, tried petting the black cat taking its ease beside her in this tension-filled room. It merely looked around and glared at her. "I don't even go out of the house here. And you think I'd have the nerve to gather up my Leica and go and do an *impersonation* in the manor house of a millionaire? God. I'd almost rather talk to the gracious Chief Superintendent Macalvie — don't tell me *he* expects me to do this?"

Jury nodded and offered her a cigarette, which she took, saying, "Thanks, it's an excuse for a drink. I don't suppose you'd care for one?"

"Try me."

Having poured the drinks into mismatched water tumblers, she sat back, raised her glass in a salute. "To your crazy idea. First of all, if you want a photographer, the Dorset police, the Devon constabulary — and Scotland Yard — must have darkrooms full of them. Why me?"

"Because they wouldn't be suspicious of you, Molly."

"I don't see why they would of a clever cop — you are trained in the lively art of worming your way into people's confidence."

It wasn't anger but pain he heard in that remark. "The people at Ashcroft would sniff out a cop all the way across Dartmoor. At least one of them would, I'm sure."

In spite of herself she was curious. "Who?"

"Better you don't know, or you'd be falling all over your tripod every time the person said Boo."

The whiskey was relaxing her. "I'd be falling all over it *anyway,* you idiot." Her raised voice disturbed the black cat. It moved, recurled itself, and gave them both a squinty gold look. "And if I don't agree to this incredible scheme — I suppose you'll blackmail me into doing it: 'Go along with us, baby, and maybe we'll go easy on you —' "

Jury laughed. It was a perfect mimicry of Macalvie's hard-boiled-detective tone.

"Thinks he's Sam Spade." She took a drink. Two. "Photos of what? What are you looking for?"

"Given the mag and Ashcroft's collection, you'd be concentrating on the cars. And the people at Ashcroft. We need some photos for identification purposes —"

"You're *police.* Just go in and take the bloody things."

"We don't have any reason to: we don't have a bit of evidence that would get us in, and it would only put everybody on guard. You wouldn't, see."

"I know I wouldn't because I won't be there. But — out of curiosity — why?"

"Because you're running scared and that timidity is going to make Ashcroft — the girl's guardian — even more courtly, and the rest will be trying to put you at your ease."

"Thanks!" she snapped, downing some more whiskey. "That sort of person hardly sounds like one a high-powered magazine would be sending out on jobs."

"They would if she had your talent.'

She lowered her head. There was no sarcasm in her voice, only defeat. "I can't do it. And I don't see any reason I should."

"I do."

"Oh, I know that old crap. 'Do it for yourself, Molly, it's what you need to —' " He could hear the tears beginning.

"No. Do it for me."

There was no sound but a log splitting and the waves beyond the window. She did not look up and did not move, but sat on the couch, feet drawn up, curled much like the cat, and just as silent.

Jury waited.

Looking not at him but at the glass she turned round and round in her hands, she said dully, "I'll need some film. I suppose this magazine wants color. Extracolor Professional or Extrachrome X." She smiled coldly. "Oh, I forgot. None of this is real, so I'll just use what I have."

"No. Treat it as if it were the real thing. Take along equipment you'd take if it *were* real."

She looked up at Jury then, still with that cold little smile, shaking her head. "Do you know the difference?" Her face turned toward the fire. "Then get me a haze filter."

He wrote it down, feeling rotten as he did.

Jury got up and went over to the couch. He leaned down, pushed back the black hair that had fallen across her face, and kissed her cheek. "Thanks, Molly."

It happened the way it had in the hotel. At one moment she was statue-still with her glass on her knee. At the next she was up and flinging it against the grate. She turned her back to him.

Jury made a move to get the glass out of the way. The cottage reeked not of whiskey, but of desolation.

"Don't bother trying to pick up the pieces."

TWENTY-FOUR

EVEN before Jess saw the passenger, she felt slightly ill just seeing the car. It was a Lamborghini. Besides the Ferrari, it was the best sports car there was. Uncle Robert had been trying to find one for years.

It was sleek, smooth, and silver. Almost the same thing could have been said about the woman who was getting out of the car, hiking an aluminum case over her shoulder. She looked so — *London*, Jessie thought. Annoyed enough about the car, must the person driving it be good-looking, too? Under the gray cape, which got in the way of the aluminum box, she wore a pearl-gray blouse and skirt and gray leather boots. It was almost as if she were choosing her clothes to match the car.

Her uncle and the rest were out. The photographer was supposed to get there at two o'clock and it was only a little past one. She was early. Jessie watched the woman come up the broad stairs and ring. Mrs. Mulchop and Jessie collided as both of them went for the door. "Now behave, for once," said Mrs. Mulchop, hand on door. "Don't be getting up to anything."

Jessie smiled benignly. The only thing she was considering

getting up to was getting the photographer in and out as quick as she could. It shouldn't take long to take pictures of a few cars.

"Hello. I'm Molly Singer," the woman said.

Mrs. Mulchop said she was sorry that Mr. Ashcroft wasn't here at the moment. He hadn't expected her until two o'clock. Would she like a cup of tea?

"If she works for a magazine," said Jessie, "she's probably got a lot of things to do. She probably doesn't have time — "

"Be quiet, child." Mrs. Mulchop gave Jess a kiss-of-death glance and repeated her offer of tea. "Or coffee, perhaps?"

"That's very kind of you. But I suppose — if you don't think Mr. Ashcroft would mind — I could get to work straightaway."

"Oh, *he* wouldn't mind at all," said Jessie. "I'll just show you where the cars are. They're outside."

Mrs. Mulchop grumbled. "I don't expect Miss Singer thought they were in the drawing room."

Molly laughed. Besides having a nice, low voice, she had a nice laugh. Nicer than Sara's. And Sara only had that old Morris Minor. . . . Jess was beginning to feel sick again. "Come on, then."

"What's your name?" asked Molly as they walked through the expanse of marble hallway, through morning room, dining room, butler's pantry (where Mulchop was topping up his glass of sherry), and kitchen.

"Jessica Allan-Ashcroft. My mother's picture is in the dining room. She led a tragic life."

"Oh, dear. How sad."

"It was, really." Jessie had stopped and taken her overall from the peg. "I always wear this when I work on the cars." She looked this new woman up and down. "You wouldn't be able to get under them, not the way you're dressed."

"Well, I hadn't planned to, actually," said Molly as they went through a dark little hallway and out to the courtyard beyond.

"It won't take you long. I'll tell you what's what and you can snap your pictures and go. My uncle has always wanted a Lamborghini. Stable at one hundred and eighty mph," she added, casually.

"You certainly do know a lot about cars." Molly had taken her thirty-five-millimeter camera from the case.

"Yes. What you could do is just get them all together if you stand back far enough and you wouldn't be wasting film."

"Not to worry. I have plenty."

Jess was afraid of that.

"Let me look them over first —"

"That one's a Ferrari; that's a Jaguar XJ-S — silent as a Rolls and does zero to sixty in under seven seconds. That one's an Aston Martin — you know, the James Bond car; there's the Porsche; this is the Lotus; this is my Mini Cooper —"

"Yours? You mean you drive it?"

"No." Jess hurried on with her description, curtailing questions. "That one's a Mercedes two-eighty-SL, a convertible. That's a —"

Molly laughed. "Hold on, there! You're going much too fast for me to remember them all."

Jess kept going. "That's a Silver Ghost, and that one's —"

"My word, a Silver Ghost. That must have cost your uncle a mint."

Jess wished she'd stop commenting so she could get on with it. "It doesn't belong to him. It's our visitor's." And then she thought of bringing in the rear-guard action. "You'd *love* him. He's an earl, like my father was. Only, of course, not that *old.* He's handsome and rich. And very nice."

"Umm."

Jessie thought her description rated more than an *umm.* But some people just couldn't be pleased. "You don't really have to know the *names* of the cars, do you, if you're only taking pictures?"

Molly adjusted the lens of the camera. "Yes, I'm afraid I

o. It wouldn't do the readers of the magazine much good to save the cars but not know what they were, would it?"

Frustrated, Jessie crossed her arms and scratched at both her elbows while she watched the photographer go about her business. She was being so careful with all of her equipment, at this rate they could be stopping here all afternoon. "What time is it?"

Molly looked at her watch. "One-thirty. If you have something you want to do, go ahead."

"No, that's all right. What about your husband? Does he take pictures too?"

"Haven't got one."

Glumly, Jessie looked her up and down again. No doubt about it, she was the best-looking one yet — all that glowing black hair and strange yellowish eyes with little flecks of brown. "Too bad."

"Not being married? You think being married's the best way to live?" Molly smiled.

"What? *No!* I think it's pretty dumb. Except for my mother and father — that was all right."

Molly fixed the camera to the unipod. "You sound like Hamlet. He said there should be no more marriages."

"I know." Mad Margaret had made an awfully fat Ophelia.

"You *do?* You must be going to a very good school if you already know Shakespeare."

"It's not school. There isn't one in spitting distance. I have tutors. They don't last long. What's that? I thought it was a cane."

Molly laughed. "I'm not quite *that* old. It's a unipod. You use it to hold the camera steady." Going through the routine might help to steady *her.* She was beginning to feel the disorientation that triggered a panic-attack out here in this unfamiliar place.

"What's that thing?" asked Jessie. She sounded worried.

"Just a spot meter. So I don't have to unthread the camera to judge the lighting or if I want a close-up."

"It sounds complicated. It sounds like it's going to take a long time. I have a camera. All I have to do is point it."

"Do you want to take some pictures?"

"No, no," said Jessie, hurriedly. "It would waste your time."

Molly was beginning to feel beads of water on her forehead. With the hand that held the spot sensor, she wiped them away. Maybe she's right. *Just take the damned picture and get the hell out*, she told herself. *Let them worry about Identikits.* She stiffened when something moved in the rear seat of the Ferrari. "What's *that*?"

"What's what? Oh, *Henry!* Don't worry, it's just Henry. He likes sleeping in cars. You look kind of pale. But Henry's safe, really. He never bit anything in his whole life. He doesn't even bite bones now, he's so old."

"I've never seen a dog like that in my entire life." Molly laughed, feeling the pressure in her mind ease up a little.

"It's just a stray we found." Jessie would never give Henry credit for his blue-blooded lineage. "He's funny-looking, isn't he?" She reached down into the Ferrari and heaved Henry out.

Molly looked up at the cirrus cloud scudding across the gray vault of endless sky and felt a wave of nausea. It always started like this, the panic-attacks. She found some tissues in her pocket and wiped the perspiration from her face.

"There's not going to be much light in a little bit. Maybe you'd rather leave and come back later. Anyway, you look kind of pale. You're not sick, are you?"

Molly had to smile over the little girl's attempt to get rid of her, though she didn't know what prompted it. The smile faded quickly, though, and she had to turn her face to the camera to keep it from cracking like a mirror. She had the unipod far enough back that she could see all ten cars together, each slotted into its box, like race-horses in their starting boxes. Irrational as it was — which made these attacks worse — she had the ugly feeling the headlamps would switch on and come racing toward her. She felt she'd been dropped into one of those silly films in which a car takes on the human potential to kill. They looked diabolical.

In this open court there was no safe place to stand. No walls, ceilings — nothing. She felt as she always did a pre-science of something awful.

"You *do* look sick."

"I'll be — all right. Just a moment . . ." Molly laid her head down on the arm supported by the unipod, and rested the other on Jessica's shoulder. The little girl put her hand over Molly's.

Even though she was out here in what seemed like an endless waste of sky and ground, Molly had the feeling of being shoved, stuffed into a dark closet where she would fall into a deep well. If only she could get back into her car —

And then she heard voices, people coming around the side of the house, laughter. People. The last thing she wanted. She was perilously near to blacking out.

Then she raised her head and saw the two men and the two women. One of the men started walking toward her, smiling. She looked at him, looked at the others, the man and the two women. Her eyes widened. She stared at this tableau vivant for a second before she felt the unipod slip beneath her weight. And she heard from what seemed a great distance, "It was Henry's fault. He scared her."

Molly Singer wanted to laugh. *Oh, the dog. The poor dog.*

When she came round, she was sitting in the Ashcroft library, being ministered to by Mrs. Mulchop with a cup of tea, Sara Millar with a cold towel, Robert Ashcroft and the other man looking concerned, and Jessica looking very guilty. It was as if her wish for release from the threat that Molly Singer represented had caused Molly's "bad spell."

Which was what Jessica was calling it as she patted her silk-sleeved arm.

"Sorry," said Molly. She put her head in her hand and tried

to laugh. "It certainly wasn't Henry's fault." She smiled at Jessica.

The man standing by Jessica's uncle was introduced as Lord Ardry. "I nearly fainted myself when I saw the Ashcroft collection." He was offering her a snifter of brandy, which she took with far more gratitude than she had the cup of tea.

"Thanks. Yes. It's quite a stunning display, but —" She had been about to say it would be better if she came back another day, and watched with a sinking heart as they seemed to be settling into chairs for a relaxing chat. Again, gratefully, she took a cigarette offered by Lord Ardry, who seemed to be observing her with more acuity than she would have liked.

"What's your magazine, Miss Singer?" asked Ashcroft. "I've forgotten."

With mounting horror, Molly knew she'd forgotten too.

"*Executive Cars,* wasn't it?" said the Earl of Caverness.

Their eyes met. He smiled. It was almost conspiratorial. What on earth did this perfect stranger know?

"Yes, that's right." She leaned back, crossed her legs, tried her best to imitate herself — the old, fairly confident Molly Singer, photographer. And very good one, too. "It's a bi-monthly. You've probably seen it."

"As a matter of fact, I haven't. I didn't think it would have much to do with the old ones. More modern-day stuff."

"No. It's got a misleading title. I keep telling them to change either the title or the image." She tried on a little laugh. It worked. Especially since the peer had given her a bit more cognac. "Let's try again, shall we. I shall try to remain upright this time."

"If you're sure — ?" Ashcroft stubbed out his cigarette. "You want me in the picture?"

He asked the question shyly.

She smiled. "Of course. *And* you, young lady."

Jessica returned the smile. The scared look had vanished

Apparently, she was willing to let Miss Singer hang around as long as she wanted, now.

Indeed, Jess went all out: "*She* has a Lamborghini."

Robert Ashcroft laughed as they trailed out of the library "Believe me, I noticed."

Maybe, thought Molly, just maybe she'd get through it

TWENTY-FIVE

THE din from the jukebox would have paralyzed any but the worst of addicts, Jury thought, when he walked into the Poor Struggler that evening. Macalvie, Wiggins, and Melrose Plant were sitting at a table in the corner.

"You've been long enough," Macalvie said to Jury.

"For what?"

"For anything," said Macalvie. "The three of us have been sitting here putting two and two together and coming up with five. Well, four-and-a-half, maybe. I bet we did better than you, Jury."

"I didn't know we were running a marathon."

"Wiggins, get the guy a drink; he looks like he could use one." Macalvie held out his hand for the holy dispensation of another Fisherman's Friend. Wiggins slid one from the packet.

Plant shook his head. "Why do you suck on those things if you think they're so vile?"

Macalvie smiled. "I tell myself every time I take one that cigarettes taste even worse." He was waving away the fra grant smoke of Plant's hand-rolled Cuban cigar. "Plant took the new governess up at Ashcroft for a ride yesterday. They went to Wynchcoombe." He turned to Melrose. "Go on. Tell him." It didn't surprise Jury that Plant had dispensed with his earldom after a few hours with Macalvie. At any rate, London had very quickly sent the fan belt (Melrose told him), and he was on the road again.

"I already have. Some of it."

Jury took out Plant's letter, and read, " 'The Earl of Curlew was also Viscount Linley, James Whyte Ashcroft. The vicar of Wynchcoombe is named Linley White. And "Clerihew" might have been "Curlew." Any connection?' It sounds like it. What did you find out?"

"He said, yes, he was some distant relation of the Ashcroft family. James Ashcroft had left the church a generous bequest. The Reverend White was surprised."

Macalvie broke in. "Someone has it in for the Ashcrofts, then? But why kill the kids? The worst possible revenge? Let me see that will."

Jury handed it over to Macalvie. "I had a talk with Simon Riley's stepmother. Maiden name — Wiggins reminded me — Elizabeth Allan. Born in County Waterford, but not much Irish blood flows through her veins or her voice."

Macalvie was silent for a moment, combing through James Ashcroft's will. Then he turned to shout over the jukebox din that if Freddie liked "Jailhouse Rock" that much, he could arrange for her to hear it from the inside. "I told you these cases were related. And I told you about Mary Mulvanney, except you still don't believe it." He grinned. "Scotland Yard, two; Macalvie, two." He looked Plant up and down. "You, one."

"Thanks," said Melrose Plant, offering Macalvie a cigar, which (to Wiggins's fright) Macalvie took.

"Robert Ashcroft, Molly Singer —"

"Mary Mulvanney," Macalvie corrected Jury automatically, eyes closed so that he could enjoy the inhalation of smoke to the maximum.

"God, Macalvie," said Jury. "You're so damned *right* all the time."

Macalvie opened his eyes. "I know."

"Sam Waterhouse. Just assume for the moment he was guilty of Rose Mulvanney's murder —"

Macalvie shook his head.

"Where is he?"

Macalvie shrugged.

Jury almost laughed. "You're the only person I know who can lie with a shrug. You're worse than Freddie. No wonder you hang around here. Why the hell don't you stop trying to protect Sam Waterhouse?"

Macalvie studied the coal-end of his cigar. "Okay. He was in here."

Jury looked at Melrose Plant. "You met him?"

Plant nodded. "It does sound as if police were looking for a scapegoat. The evidence against him was pretty circumstantial. You think so, too, don't you?"

"I don't know. But I certainly think the evidence against Molly Singer is circumstantial."

"Mary Mulvanney." Macalvie's kneejerk response.

"How'd she do at Ashcroft?" Jury asked Melrose.

"Miss Singer? Incredibly well —"

"She's no more phobic than I am," said Macalvie generously.

Melrose Plant smiled. "I'd be careful with comparisons if I were you, Mr. Macalvie."

"So we've got the pictures, so what have we got? Yeah, there *was* an advert. Robert Ashcroft went to see a Roller in Hampstead Heath." Macalvie stuffed a couple of Plant's cigars in his pocket before he got up. "The hell with it. It's time we had a little talk with Robert Ashcroft."

On his way out, Macalvie kicked the jukebox and "Don't Be Cruel."

II

"Mr. Ashcroft," said Macalvie, "you usually interview potential tutors or governesses or whatever you call them at home, don't you?"

There was a decanter of whiskey at his elbow, and Macalvie had no hesitation in helping himself. It went down well with Plant's cigars.

"That's right." Robert Ashcroft looked from Macalvie to Jury to Wiggins taking notes. He frowned. "I'm sorry. I don't —"

Macalvie made a sign with his hand that Ashcroft didn't have to understand a damned thing. Yet. "But this time you went to London to interview the applicants."

Ashcroft smiled. It was an easy smile. "I decided it might be better. I believe I'd misjudged my niece's ability to make the final choice."

"The lady Jessica not being such a hot judge of character?"

Ashcroft's smile was even more disarming. "On the contrary, a wonderful judge. She always chose the one least suitable."

Macalvie frowned. "As a governess?"

"No. As a wife. Jess is afraid I'm going to be snagged by Jane Eyre."

"With you as Rochester," said Macalvie. "So you're not in danger of marriage, then?"

"I never thought of marriage as 'dangerous.' Are you suggesting some sexual leaning? That every couple of months I go up to London to indulge my perverse tastes?"

Macalvie turned the cigar round and round in his mouth. "We weren't thinking particularly of you down in your lab drinking something that would turn you into Hyde, no."

"Superintendent — "

"Chief." Macalvie smiled.

"I beg your pardon. Are you still upset about that crazy ruse of Jess's that brought you all out here?"

"Hell, no. Kids will be kids, won't they?" His smile flickered less like the flame than the moth. "You stayed at the Ritz, right? On the tenth to the fifteenth?"

"Yes. What's that — ?"

"You interviewed several applicants for this post."

Robert Ashcroft nodded, frowning.

"What else did you do?"

"Nothing much. Went to see a Rolls-Royce in Hampstead But it wasn't what I wanted."

"And — ?"

Ashcroft had risen from the sofa and gone to toss his cigarette into the fireplace. The picture of his brother hung over him. Jury wondered how heavily. "I went to the theater and the Tate. Walked round Regent's Park and Piccadilly. What's this all about?"

"What'd you see?"

Ashcroft's bewilderment turned to anger. "Pigeons."

"Funny. The play, I mean."

"*The Aspern Papers.* Vanessa Redgrave."

"Good?"

"No. I walked out."

Macalvie put on his surprised and innocent look. "You walked out on Vanessa Redgrave?"

"I didn't exactly throw her over for another woman."

"I don't imagine many people walked out."

"I wasn't checking. Except my coat," Ashcroft said, acidly.

"So since probably *no one* would walk out on Vanessa, I bet the cloakroom attendant would remember you."

Ashcroft was furious. "What in the hell is this about, Chief Superintendent Macalvie?"

"What was at the Tate?"

"Pictures."

It wasn't as easy to unnerve Ashcroft as Jury thought.

"Mr. Ashcroft, would you try not playing this for laughs? What was at the Tate?"

"The Pre-Raphaelities."

Macalvie was silent, turning the cigar.

"Ever heard of them?"

"Rossetti and that bunch. I've heard. Why didn't you drive to London with all those cars sitting around out there?"

"For the obvious reason. I thought I'd be buying a car — the Rolls."

Jury sat there, smoking, saying nothing.

Robert Ashcroft had an answer for everything. And Macalvie knew it.

TWENTY-SIX

"THAT'S it for tonight, then." Sara slapped the book shut. Jessie, whose bed they were lying on, since she refused her nightly story in the Laura Ashley room, had been getting so drowsy her head had nearly drifted onto Sara's arm. Quickly, she snapped out of it. To have Sara think she was actually cozying up to her would be dreadful. "You've left off at the best part. Where Heathcliff is carrying Cathy's dead body around."

"You do put things in the most morbid way."

"*I* didn't write it, did I?" said Jess, reasonably. She felt as if Sara had reprimanded her, no matter how mildly. Jess gave Henry (who was lying at the bottom of the bed) a little kick. If *she* was being scolded, then Henry would have to come in for his share of it. What was really bothering her was that, against her will — and *that* would require a strong force indeed — she was afraid she might begin to *like* Sara. The Selfless Sara. Jessie sighed. But she didn't think she liked her as much as that lady photographer. Maybe it was because the one named Molly had fears, just as Jess had, only they wouldn't admit it.

It was an awful dilemma, liking someone you wanted to hate, the worst dilemma since the ax-murderer call to police. All of that blood in her mind had become so vivid it might have been really running down the walls. She shuddered.

"What's the matter?" asked Sara.

"Nothing." Jessie picked up the glossy magazine Molly Singer had given her. *Executive Cars.*

Sara was saying something about Heathcliff. "I thought you thought he was so romantic."

Romance? How disgusting. Better to imagine murderers stalking her (and Henry) across the moor. Green, green bogs with liverworts and moss, like Cranmere Pool, and peat, and rush ground where you could be sucked down, your head just dangling, as if guillotined, your little hand (and Henry's paw), the last thing to disappear from the sight of all those gathered round, throwing ropes, calling to you. . . .

"Romance is stupid."

Sara hit her lightly over the head with the book. "You're the one asked me to read it." Sara sat up suddenly, her back rigid. "What was that?"

"What was what?" Jessie was looking at a picture of a Lamborghini, newer than Molly's. Twenty thousand pounds. Maybe Mr. Mack —

"It sounded like a car. Down the drive."

Jessie yawned, her eyes getting heavy. "Maybe it's Uncle Rob and Victoria coming back." She thought her uncle had been awfully moody at dinner. Victoria got him to go out for a drive and a drink at a new pub several miles away. Maybe Victoria would worm out of him what was wrong. Her eyes snapped open.

Victoria, Jessie realized suddenly, was rather good at getting her uncle in a better frame of mind. She frowned and thought about that.

"It's too early for them to be back," said Sara.

Now Sara looked moody and worried. What was the *matter*

with everyone? "I want hot chocolate and toast. Come on, Henry."

Moody himself, Henry clambered down off the bed.

II

Jess sat at the kitchen table, turning the pages of *Executive Cars,* while the kettle for tea and the pan of milk for chocolate heated on the hob. Sara got out the granary loaf to cut and toast. "I wish the Mulchops were here," she said.

The Mulchops had gone to Okehampton to visit some relative or other. "Them? Whatever for?"

Sara shrugged. "I just feel — edgy."

Jess slapped over another page, annoyed. "Well, *they* wouldn't be any help. I mean if some ghost was walking around or something."

"Stop talking like that."

Jess shrugged. Sara was spoiling one of Jess's favorite times. The kitchen chill around the edges, but nice and warm right here by the fire, without Mrs. Mulchop bustling and kneading dough and Mulchop slopping down soup and giving Jessie evil looks. He didn't like her, she knew, because she got under the cars.

Probably because she was "edgy," Sara started humming to herself, and then singing while she sliced the bread. She must have thought ghosts and vampires and werewolves ran away when they heard old Irish tunes. Jess glanced up when she heard "... *when she was dead, and laid in grave ...*"

"That's 'Barbara Allan.'"

Sara looked stricken. "Oh, I'm sorry. Really. I suppose it's because I hear so much about your mother —" She stopped, staring toward the kitchen door, the one that led out to the courtyard. "There *is* a noise out there."

This time Jess heard it too. A sort of scraping sound. But the wind was getting higher, and one of the stable doors banged; the sound could have been anything. "It's just the horses." She really wished Sara weren't such a mouse about things. It was just like the wife in *Rebecca*. She thrust that thought from her mind.

Sara went back to cutting the bread, and just as suddenly stopped. "It sounds like footsteps." She listened intently, shook her head, went back to the bread.

Well, it *had* sounded like footsteps, but Jess refused to give in. "It's just Henry; sometimes he scrapes his paw in his sleep." Henry never moved *anything* in his sleep, as Jess knew perfectly well.

She went on looking at the cars. Daimlers, Rollers, Ferraris . . next page, another Daimler and some cheaper cars, but still collector's items. Beside the black Daimler was a little Morris Minor, vintage.

The Daimler . . . she kept her eyes averted because they were filling with tears. Her father James had been taken to the cemetery in a Daimler. And once again the graveyard scene sprang up, as if it were yesterday, and she saw herself standing beside the grave. The mourners — thick-veiled women, black-suited men. Her uncle had been the only spot of light in that dark-shrouded world.

That Daimler had had a *Y* registration. Jess blushed from remembering having noticed, even in her grief, the registration on the funereal Daimler. And then her skin went cold.

She turned back to the page before. Morris Minor. Black. *R* registration. Jess's thoughts stopped suddenly, braking. It must be what an animal feels, maybe even Henry. The thoughts stop. Senses take over. You see, you hear, you feel fright. . . .

What she heard, and Sara, too, given the knife had stopped slicing bread, was the creaking in the kitchen entry. Sara's face was pale, looking toward the door that, when Jess had nerved herself to look around, was opening.

Molly Singer stood there in her silvery cape, white-faced,

black-haired. In her fright, Jess almost thought she *was* see-ing a ghost.

Except that this ghost was holding a gun in her black-gloved hand.

Despite all of this, the only thing that Jess could see in her mind's eye was a black Daimler and a Morris Minor. *R* regis-tration. Not vintage.

She stared at Molly Singer and then back at the kitchen table, where an entire loaf of bread lay sliced, and wondered, what had Sara Millar's car been doing at her father's funeral?

II

Five miles away in the Help the Poor Struggler, Macalvie was still arguing that Ashcroft had gone about the whole in-terviewing business in a damned peculiar way.

Melrose Plant was drinking Old Peculier and smoking. And wondering about Robert Ashcroft's "interviews."

"He could have left that play *deliberately* so he'd establish that he'd been in London. How many people walk out on *Vanessa?*" asked Macalvie.

Wiggins said, "The cloakroom attendant recognized the picture immediately. No luck yet though with the car lots. But we've only had a few hours." He made a bit of a produc-tion of unzipping a box of lozenges to call the divisional com-mander's attention to the fact that Macalvie was smoking. Again.

"And why didn't he call home? Gone for five days and not a word back to his beloved niece," Macalvie went on, looking from Plant to Jury, irritated that he seemed to be arguing without an opponent.

"It was coincidence that the note to Jessica went under the rug. A coincidence with wretched consequences, unfortu-nately. Wasn't it the same thing Angel Clare did?" asked Jury.

"Who the hell's Angel Clare?" asked Macalvie.

Melrose Plant looked at him. "Commander, if you were hiring a tutor, you'd damned well make sure he or she was extremely well read, wouldn't you?"

Macalvie gave him an especially magical Macalvie-smile. "If you need a tutor, Plant, I'm sorry I don't come up to your standards."

"Ah, but you do. Superintendent Jury told me the pre-Raphaelites held for you no horrors. Nor did *Jane Eyre*. What about Hester and Chillingworth?"

Macalvie cadged a cigar and looked at Plant as if he'd gone mad. "What the hell is this? A literary quiz?"

"In a way."

"*The Scarlet Letter.* So what?"

Plant shrugged. "I'd just think any tutor would —"

"*Tess of the D'Urbervilles*," said Jury, absently. He looked very pale and was getting out of his chair. "My God, all of this time and we forgot —"

He made for the telephone in the middle of the heartrending voice of Elvis singing "Heartbreak Hotel."

It was one of the last songs Elvis Presley had sung.

III

At first, when Molly Singer said the name, Jess thought she was talking to her. But then she said it again.

"Let her go, Tess."

Jessie knew what real fear was as the arm tightened around her shoulders and the knife nearly bit into her throat. Sara — but was that her real name? — whispered, "Get out! *Who are you?*"

"Mary."

The arm moved up, nearly cutting off Jessica's wind. She wanted to cry but she couldn't. Where, where, was everybody? She heard Henry whine. Henry knew she was in trouble.

The flat, now unfamiliar voice of the young woman choking her was saying, "I don't know you. I don't know you."

"But I know you, Tess." Molly's voice wavered, but the gun-hand didn't. "I took some pictures. Of the Marine Parade. I had one of them blown up because there was something familiar about the girl in the picture. It might be years since I've seen you, but I'd know you anywhere, anywhere. You always looked like Mum, even when you were little."

It was as though Sara didn't hear her. "Put down the gun or I'll cut her up right now, right here. I was waiting for him to come back, damn him and all the Ashcrofts. It has to be here in the kitchen. I'll write him a message in her blood. . . . *He killed Mum, don't you realize that?* They were there in the house together. And then I came down in the morning . . ."

This was coming out in gasps, and Jess felt tears on the top of her head, on her hair. But the knife was still there, sharply honed, edge now against her chest. "So you've got to put down the gun, Mary."

Jess could see the gun shake in the hand of Molly Singer. *Don't let her have it, please, please.* She would have cried it out, but the arm was like a steel band around her shoulders. And then, in despair, she watched Molly drop the gun. The sound when it hit the floor flooded Jess with terror.

Sara was shoving Jess toward the kitchen table, whispering to her, or to Molly, that it was just the sacrifice, you see, of Isaac. It had to be done. Like the others. "Only I didn't have to cut the others up."

"And you're not going to do it to Jessica, either."

It was another voice, a man's.

Jess felt the knife move away from her, the obstructing arm torn from her shoulders and the voice saying, *Run, Jess.*

She ran toward the little hall.

But then she remembered Henry. Jess ran back, bunched

him in her arms, and flew out the door into the shielding darkness of the night.

The rage of Teresa Mulvanney made her faster than either of them. She was out of his grasp and sliding across the floor to grab at the gun before Molly's hand could get to it.

Tess Mulvanney whipped the gun around, and from where she lay on the floor she shot Sam Waterhouse.

Molly opened her mouth to scream. But she didn't. Instead, she tried to inch her way to the table where lay the knife and the load of cut-up bread. She tried to talk to her sister, while tears slid down her face. "Tess. That's Sammy. Don't you remember? You loved him —"

Teresa's eyes widened. "It's not." As she closed her eyes, as if in an effort of remembrance, Molly took another step nearer the table. "They put him away. I read about the trial a year ago. When I got out of hospital. Everybody lied — *don't touch that!*"

Molly had almost had her hand on the knife when her sister grabbed it up. She raised the gun and slowly lowered it again. The look of rage turned to emotions confused and more gentle. "Mary." Tears ran down her face. "Don't you understand that I should've saved her? I should've saved Mum. If only I'd been brave enough to stab him, but I didn't know what —" She looked at the knife in her hand and let it fall on the floor. Tess ran the hand holding the gun across her wet forehead, but when Molly edged toward her, she steadied the hand again and shook her head violently. "Good-bye, Mary."

And she was out the door, the same one Jess had run through carrying Henry.

Molly knelt by Sam. The bullet had caught him in the side. His eyes were closed and she was terrified. But then he came round. Blood was seeping through his fingers. "I'm okay. But for God's sakes, get Teresa. Or she'll be back —" Sam passed out.

Molly could see, through the kitchen window, a path of light cut by a torch. Then she heard a car door slam.

Teresa couldn't afford to stop to look for Jessie out there in the dark; Robert Ashcroft could come driving up at any moment —

And then she remembered the Lamborghini.

Molly ran through the house, out the front door, down the drive toward her car. She heard, way off behind her, the distant sound of another car starting up.

There was only one way out of Ashcroft.

IV

"Heartbreak Hall," said Jury. "That's what you called it." Jury had his coat on.

Macalvie stared at him and got up. So did Plant and Wiggins.

It was the first time Divisional Commander Macalvie had looked ashen and unsure of himself. Or was at a loss for words. But he finally found them as the four men headed for the door. "God, Jury. Not *Teresa Mulvanney*. I forgot to check out Tess —"

"*We* forgot, Brian. The forgotten little girl. You told me about Mary Mulvanney coming into your office. She said she couldn't stand to go back there again. According to Harbrick Hall, Teresa Mulvanney appeared to be coming out of it, like someone coming out of a fugue state. That was six years ago. Over the next year her improvement was miraculous. They gave her jobs to do. She did them well. She was articulate, well-behaved, calm. And it was a Lady Pembroke, charitable old dame, who told them she'd take over the care of Teresa Mulvanney."

"Let's get the hell out of here. Macalvie turned to Melrose "You mind if we use your car, pal? Mine won't go from zero to ten in under an hour."

There was an apprehensive glance from Wiggins when

Melrose handed the keys over. "This one will go a little faster."

That was an understatement, or so Macalvie proved it to be. Wiggins was hunched down as far as possible in the back seat. The narrow road, the occasional thick hedges, the night, the murderous moor-mist, all contrived to make driving nearly impossible.

Macalvie didn't seem to notice as he careened the Rolls around a turn. "How did she know? How on earth could she hand-pick her victims like that?"

"Pitifully simple. As I said to Mr. Mack, a will that's been probated is in the public domain. Sara Millar–Teresa Mulvanney simply looked at the heirs to the Ashcroft fortune. As far as George Thorne was concerned, well, she might have thought of him as — who knows, a conspirator. And there was also the simple matter of geography. The final object was Jessica. The others she killed . . . on the way." Jury felt sick.

Macalvie scraped the left-hand fender cutting the curve of a stone wall too sharply. "Sorry, friend."

Melrose, smoking calmly in the back seat, said, "I can always get parts."

He hit the steering wheel again and again with the heel of his hand. "But goddamnit, Jury! They were kids! Why the hell didn't she just go after Ashcroft if he's the one who murdered Rose Mulvanney?"

"She couldn't."

Macalvie took his eyes off the road for a crucial second and the fender got it again. "What the hell do you mean?"

"He was already dead."

V

It was a long driveway, a drive like a tunnel, and Molly could hear the car, which must have been coming round the side of the house. She didn't yet see the headlamps.

She started to switch on the Lamborghini's lights, and paused. Tess could easily think it was Robert Ashcroft returning and head right into him. Molly found she had at least a little interest in living, which surprised her. There might be a way to stop Teresa without actually killing herself.

Something to take her by surprise, make her veer off into the thick trees, maybe an accident, but not a fatal one. The camera equipment. Flashbulbs? Not enough bulbs, not enough time. And now when she looked up she saw, at the end of the tunnel, far off, the headlamps of Tess's car.

The light at the end of the tunnel / Is the light of an oncoming train. . . . The lines of Lowell suddenly came back to her. She snatched the unipod from the rear seat, smashed out the right-hand headlamp, tossed the thing in the back and got in. Was there anything more disconcerting to a driver than to see only one light coming toward him rather than two? What was it? Car? Motorbike? And the moment of confusion —

The other car was halfway down the drive, its lights hazy in the middle distance. Molly started the engine and headed up the drive. *Ah, hell. You only die once.*

They weren't more than a dozen yards apart, when the wheels of the Morris screeched and the car swerved and rammed into the wall. Then it went into a spin and rammed the front of the Lamborghini.

The Rolls was only a minute away from the Ashcroft drive when they heard the sound of tearing metal.

Macalvie jammed on the brakes at the entrance. The four of them piled out.

The Morris burst into flames as they ran.

Molly's car was a disaster, but it wasn't burning. It was a distance from the flaming Morris, and it was tougher.

And for the seconds it took Macalvie to pull her out of the wreckage, so was Molly Singer.

Blood trickled from her ear, and a tiny line of blood ran

from the corner of her mouth. But she did not look bruised or broken. She looked up at Macalvie, who was holding her in his arms. She smiled. "Damnit. Why do you *always* have to be right, Mac——?" She didn't get out the last of it. The long fingers that clutched his shoulder slid down his coat as slowly as a hand playing a harp.

Macalvie started shaking her and shouting: *"Mary!"* He shouted the name until Jury pulled him away.

Melrose Plant took off his coat and put it under her head. Jury took off his own coat and covered her with it.

A trickle of gas from the Morris reached the Lamborghini. All Jury could think of was the log falling and sparking in Molly Singer's cottage.

TWENTY-SEVEN

JURY found her on the mechanic's creeper under the Zimmer. She was holding on tight to Henry.

Jessica did not want to come out.

"Please, Jessie. It's all over. It's okay now."

Okay. It would never be okay, not for Divisional Commander Macalvie. He had disappeared into the trees and the fog.

"It's better here," said Jess. There was a silence. "I don't want to get cut up. And I don't want Henry to, either."

Jury sat down, there on the cold stone of the courtyard, cold as hell himself without his coat. She was silent. "Was Sara the ax-murderer?"

"No. There was never an ax-murderer, Jess. Sara —" He didn't know whether to tell her or not, then decided he might as well level. "Sara was sick, very sick. She was the one who killed the children."

"But why me? Was she their governess too?"

"No. No, she wasn't. Why you? Because she was confused. A long time ago, much longer than before you were born, someone hurt her and she wanted revenge. Someone killed her mother. You can see how terrible that would be."

"But *we* didn't do it — I mean me and Davey and that other boy and girl! Stop it, Henry! Henry doesn't like it under here, but I'm afraid something will happen to him."

She was crying, Jury could hear. "Nothing can possibly happen."

"Well, he'd rather be *in* the car than under it. So you put him up in the seat. But don't let him *go* anywhere." She said it pretty fiercely, as if she wanted to be sure, now Jury was there, that he stayed.

"Come on, Henry," said Jury. He lugged the dog out and put him in the front seat of the Zimmer. Henry shook himself and seemed to open his eyes. A new world. Strange, but new.

And strange and new for Jessica Ashcroft too. "Well?"

"Sorry. Well, what?"

"You didn't answer my question. We didn't kill her mother."

"I know."

"*Well?*"

Jury thought she must be getting better. She was certainly testier. "Let me tell you something that's very — difficult to understand, Jess. I think what was wrong with Sara was she felt guilty. She was only five when her mother died. And she *saw* it." Jury stopped for a moment. He remembered his conversation with Mrs. Wasserman, how he'd asked, without thinking, what the bolted door kept out. Him. To Mrs. Wasserman all the fears were focused on Him. Displacement, whatever a psychiatrist might have called it. "I think Sara felt, well, horribly guilty —"

From under the sanctuary of the dark car, Jessica said. "I know. She thought it was her fault. She thought she did it. And maybe she thought she was killing her own self when she killed Davey and that girl. And almost me."

He could hardly believe his ears. Until he heard her crying

again, and then realized how much guilt she must have felt about the death of the most beautiful, the kindest woman Jessica had ever imagined, yet never known. And how she could easily have felt responsible. Barbara Allan had died so soon after her daughter was born.

Jury could think of nothing to say.

"How is that man who saved me?"

"He's fine; the ambulance just got here to take him to hospital."

She rolled out. She got off the creeper. Her nightdress, her face, her hair were smudged with oil and grease. "Come on, Henry," she said, her tone its usual testy self.

Henry clambered out of the car and followed them as they walked slowly across the courtyard. Jessie was holding Jury's hand.

"I'll tell you something," she said grumpily.

"Yes? What?"

"I hope I never run up against Jane Eyre."

II

When Robert Ashcroft and Victoria Gray were driving, a few minutes later, toward home, they heard the sirens, saw the whirring lights, saw the fire in the driveway.

"Oh, God, oh, God," whispered Victoria.

Robert Ashcroft gunned the Ferrari up to seventy.

He jumped out of the car, threaded his way through police and ambulance crew, and ran in the house calling for his niece.

Jury had never seen a man look so terrified, with one exception, and then so relieved. No exception there.

Jessica stood, hands on hips, grease-smudged face and oil-bedewed hair, glaring up at her uncle. "I don't want any more governesses. Until I go away to school, I want a bodyguard. I want that man that saved my life."

Ashcroft merely nodded. He had tears in his eyes.

"Come on, Henry." They climbed the stairs slowly. But halfway up she turned to deliver her parting shot.

"You're always away when the ax-murderers come." Then she and Henry continued their weary ascent.

VII

Pretty
Molly Brannigan

TWENTY-EIGHT

THE old char was singing in Wynchcoombe church and wringing her mop in a pail. Out of deference either to Jury or the vicar's lad who'd been buried only yesterday, she stopped singing and kept on swabbing the floor.

Death did not stop the stone from getting dirty or flowers from wilting, and the ones on the altar looked in need of changing. He watched her running the grubby mop over the stone floor and wondered how something that made such an enormous difference to so many — all of those deaths — could make little more than a dent in the daily round of cleaning.

The old woman with the mop and pail paid no attention to him, one of the many who came to see this little marvel of a church that towered cathedral-like over its valley in the moor.

Jury dropped some money in the collection box, listening to the charwoman, who couldn't resist her bit of music, change to humming. He thought of Molly Singer and imagined that somewhere in Waterford or Clare or Donegal, a clear-voiced Irish girl might be doing her washing-up, maybe humming from the boredom of it

Damn it, why are you always right, Mac?

Jury looked at the painting of Abraham and Isaac, the knife near the terrified boy's face. His father ready for the sacrifice. All God had to do was say *Go.*

To Macalvie, who had been right all along about her, she was Mary Mulvanney.

To Jury, she would always be Molly Singer.

He felt the old char watching him as he walked out of the church.

II

When he got to the Help the Poor Struggler, it was almost a relief to hear Divisional Commander Macalvie shouting over the noise of the jukebox that he'd tie Freddie to a tree in Wistman's Wood if she didn't stop singing along with Elvis. It was the version of "Are You Lonesome Tonight?" where Elvis forgot the words and was laughing at himself and the audience was joining in. What rapport, thought Jury, Elvis Presley had had with his audience. It was a song he must have sung a hundred times, yet he'd forgotten — probably because of his failing powers — the words. But his fans hadn't. They never would. There were some things people never forgot. Like his last concert.

"Y'r a rate trate, no mistake. He be dead, man. Hain't yuh got no respect fer the dead?"

Macalvie was silent for a moment. Then he shouted back, "If I did, Freddie, I'd have some respect for *you.* Hullo," he added grudgingly to Jury. Melrose Plant was sitting with Macalvie. It was a drunk Brian Macalvie. "How about one of your fancy cigars, friend?" he said to Plant. And to Wiggins, who had opened his mouth, Macalvie said, "Shut up."

Freddie, who must have heard something and was being halfway human to Macalvie, set his pint on the table and said to Wiggins — or all of them — "No use to argie-fy with Ma-calvie."

"How's Sam?" asked Jury.

"Fine. He's fine. Be out of hospital in a couple of weeks." Macalvie smoked and stared at his pint.

"How'd he know, Brian? That Jessica might be in danger?"

Turning his glass round and round, Macalvie said, "The bloody coat-of-arms. The letter Plant wrote to you. That and the picture. You remember, he went through her desk. The unidentified man. Sammy saw Robert Ashcroft at the George in Wynchcoombe. James and Robert looked a lot alike. At first he thought Robert was simply a man who looked a hell of a lot like the one in Rose's snap. It was seeing the coat-of-arms that he'd seen on a piece of notepaper in the desk that finally did it. Anyway, he thought he should keep an eye on Ashcroft."

"You were right. There *was* something he knew that hadn't surfaced. James Ashcroft was indiscreet, writing to Rose Mulvanney."

"To say the least. He let Sammy waste his life in prison. Bastard."

Plant said, "I think Robert Ashcroft will try and make up for that in some way."

Macalvie glared at him. "Buy him a car, maybe. Sam told me he watched that house from a spot on the moor where he set up camp. He figured something would happen." Another silence. "It happened."

A big, beefy man was plugging money into the jukebox. "Play a few Golden Oldies, or something, you will?" yelled Macalvie.

The perfect stranger looked around, and not in a friendly way. "Play what I like, mate." He rippled muscles as best he could under the leather jacket. "Who the hell you be, any-way?"

Macalvie started to get up.

Jury pulled him down. "Forget it, Brian."

Having to yell at someone, Macalvie turned again to Freddie. "Bring us four more and try and keep the tapwater out of it this time."

"A course, me 'anzum," said Freddie, over the double-din of the music and the casuals off the road. Considering the usual lack of custom, the pub was almost jumping. Even the dartboard was getting a workout.

And then an Irish voice from the jukebox, thin and silvery, was singing. Apparently, leather-jacket was a sentimentalist.

> *"O, man, dear, did ya never hear*
> *Of pretty Molly Brannigan —"*

The cigar stopped halfway to Macalvie's mouth. His expression was blank.

> *"She's gone away and left me,*
> *And I'll never be a man again —"*

Macalvie had taken out his wallet and checked the contents. "Being an earl," he said to Melrose, "and probably owning a big hunk of England, I don't suppose you'd be good for a loan of, say, eighty quid, would you?"

Without any questions, Melrose took out his money clip, peeled off four twenties, and handed them over.

> *". . . Now that Molly's gone and left me*
> *Here for to die."*

Macalvie walked over to the bar where Freddie was singing along and spread a hundred and thirty pounds in front of her.

> *"Oh, the left side of me heart*
> *Is as weak as watered gruel, man;*
> *Won't ye come to me wake*
> *when I make that great meander, man. . . ?"*

Freddie, watching him, shouted, " 'Ere, Mac, wot be yu on upon?"

Macalvie had already positioned himself, taken aim, and shoved his size ten straight into the jukebox.

The song splintered like a broken windscreen, flying into pieces, shivers of metal and glass. It caught the entire room in a freeze-frame. No one moved.

Except Macalvie, who walked back to his chair and snatched up his coat. He looked around the table and said, "Macalvie, nil. Mulvanney, nil."

Then he turned with his coat slung over his shoulder and walked out into the dark where, not far away, the prison rose through the mists of Dartmoor and hung over Princetown like a huge raven.

Match wits with Richard Jury of Scotland Yard. And solve these cunning murders by

_____	The Anodyne Necklace	10280-4-35	$3.50
_____	The Dirty Duck	12050-0-13	3.50
_____	The Man With A Load		
_____	Of Mischief	15327-1-13	3.50
_____	The Old Fox Deceiv'd	16747-7-21	3.50
_____	Jerusalem Inn	14181-8-11	3.95